Wild at Heart

Wilder Irish, book four

Mari Carr

ISBN: 978-1-950870-09-7

Editor: Kelli Collins

Cover artist: Melissa Gill Designs

Print formatting: Mari Carr

Wilder Irish, book 4: April

Fiona has a man problem—she has too many in her life. How does she choose between Owen, the sweet boy (turned sexy man) she dated in college and Asher, the hot hunk starring in too many current fantasies?

Fiona's resigned to having neither man…until Owen and Asher take matters into their own hands—literally. It's a case of life imitating sexy sitcom…even more so when Fiona's recent ex, Mr. Big Gesture himself, shows up to win her back—with his biggest gesture yet.

Dedication

This story is dedicated to my sprinting buddies.
Without Lexi Blake, Lila Dubois, Shelli Stevens, Erin Nicholas,
Erin McCarthy and Bianca D'Arc,
I'd never finish a damn book.

Special Acknowledgements go to Lexi for "Happy Clam"
and Lila for the stellar tagline.
It's good to have friends with dirty minds.

Prologue

Patrick Collins looked up from his book and tried to hide a smile as his five-year-old granddaughter flittered into the living room in a long yellow ball gown. The outfit was a far cry from the T-shirt and shorts he'd put her to bed in not more than twenty minutes earlier. "I thought you were taking a wee nap, Fiona."

Fiona Adams shook her head. "No. I'm not tired. We're going to have a dance."

"I see." Patrick put the bookmark in place to mark his spot and lowered the leg rest on his recliner. "So, no nap?"

Patrick wasn't surprised, and he figured his daughter, Teagan, wouldn't be too upset with him for failing to get the young child to sleep. It was obvious when she'd suggested he put Fiona down for an hour or so, Teagan had no expectation of his success.

Fiona rolled her eyes. "Babies take naps. I'm not a baby. I'm Belle."

"Well, you certainly do look like the belle of the ball. Is that the dress your cousin Caitie gave you earlier?"

Fiona held it out and curtsied. "It fits."

He recalled Fiona's delight as she went through the bag of hand-me-downs Keira had dropped by earlier in the day. His kids had grown up passing down their clothes—pretty much a necessity when raising seven of them—and they'd always felt the same excitement as they'd tried on the "new" old clothes. Fiona nearly had a conniption when she'd come across the Belle dress, ready to change immediately, but Teagan had tucked it aside, telling her daughter she could try it on later.

Patrick understood now why it had been so easy for him to get her to lay down. She'd wanted easy, uninterrupted access to the dress they'd tucked away in the bedroom.

She walked closer to him. "You're the beast."

Patrick chuckled. "I've been called worse, I suppose. As I recall, your cousin made me play this role when she was wearing that dress as well."

Fiona took his hand, drawing him up and over to the old record player in the corner. He'd had the thing for close to forty years and Fiona was enthralled by it. Nowadays, it was only used a few times a year, most of those when Fiona was visiting.

The rest of the year, she spent on her parents' tour bus, traveling around the country as they performed shows in so many cities in the U.S., he'd lost count.

Sky Mitchell and Teagan Collins.

Fiona's parents had run into each other in the pub just over a decade ago and since then, they'd taken the world by storm with their music. While Fiona's older sister, Ailis, didn't seem quite as fond of the constant motion, Fee took to it like a fish to water. She was inquisitive, vivacious, and energetic. Or to quote her tired mother when she'd dropped her off this morning, "Precocious as hell. Hide your credit cards and anything else you value."

"Play that dancing-girl song."

Patrick tried to figure out what she meant, but he drew a blank. "Dancing girl?"

Fiona gave him a rather impatient look as if what she wanted should be obvious. "You played it last time. I think her name is Manilla."

"Ah," the light went on. "'Waltzing Matilda'."

"That's it. Play that one."

Patrick didn't have a clue what it was about that song she'd remembered. He had found an album of children's songs in a secondhand shop a year earlier and bought it to play for Fiona's visit, knowing how she loved the record player. She'd made him play that particular song no less than twenty times, always giggling as she sang along.

He flipped through the albums until he found it, then pulled the record from the sleeve. "Are you sure this is appropriate music for your ball? I thought Belle and the Beast danced to something else."

Fiona rolled her eyes, something she appeared to do quite a lot whenever she felt the adults around her were saying something ridiculous. He'd heard Sky trying to explain to her just last night at dinner that it wasn't polite, but when Fiona persistently questioned him about why, fielding all his answers with more questions, the lecture quickly failed. Tris had pointed to her and quietly commented that, "Teagan and Sky have their hands full with that one," while Riley leaned over and proclaimed Fiona, "the coolest kid ever."

"It's ball music because it's slow and I need you to twirl me. See?" She spun in a circle, her yellow dress flowing outwards in a pretty fan.

"I understand." Patrick started to put the needle down, but Fiona pushed closer.

"Can I do that?"

The last time he'd deemed her too young, worried about her scratching the record or breaking the needle. He suspected he wouldn't win that argument again. "You remember you have to do it carefully."

She nodded earnestly. "I'll be careful." She lifted the arm and together they counted out the three lines that indicated where her song started. True to her word, she lowered it very gently, holding in her excitement when the music began playing until she'd backed away from the player, so as not to jar it.

Fiona took his arm, and they did a rather frenzied jig that involved a lot of spinning on her part as he held her hands. He wasn't sure how she didn't get dizzy, but it was clear from the sheer joy on her face, she was in her element.

"Play it again," she cried out when the music stopped.

They took Matilda out for three more waltzes before Fiona started to slow down.

"I love to dance."

"So do I," Patrick said when the song ended again. "Used to cut a rug with your grandma Sunday in this living room all the time."

Fiona glanced at the floor, confused. "Why did you cut the rug? Where?"

He laughed, and the two of them collapsed onto the couch to catch their breath. "It's an expression. It means dancing."

"Cut a rug," she repeated. No doubt she'd be pulling that out to use on her parents later. Patrick was very impressed with the young girl's vocabulary. Teagan said she was a voracious reader, several grade levels ahead of most five-year-olds.

She turned to face him on the couch, her cheeks red from dancing. Fiona and her sister shared their mother's auburn hair and porcelain skin. Her bright blue eyes took in everything, expressed everything.

"I swear you are the spit of your mother, Fiona."

She considered that, then—clever girl—said, "You said that last time I was here. It means I look like her."

He grinned. "It does. You have your mother's looks and your father's personality." While Teagan and little Ailis were quiet and more introspective, Fiona and Sky tended to take over a room. Not in a bad way. They just had these larger-than-life personalities that drew attention. He'd noticed it last night when the grandchildren were playing after dinner. Though she was younger than several of her cousins, Fiona seemed to drive the action, the older kids following her suggestions because they were fun. In fact, fun appeared to follow the young girl. She was creative and clever, quick to laugh, and always telling silly jokes that had all the adults in stitches.

"Your name suits you."

"My name?" she asked.

"Fiona. It means fair."

Fiona sighed and shook her head. "That doesn't fit at all."

He frowned. "What do you mean?"

"My mom said so." Fiona adopted a tone he suspected was her imitating her mother. "She always says, 'You're not playing fair, Fiona. You have to share your toys with Ailis.' Even when I don't want to."

Patrick worked overtime to school his features, certain his daughter probably did use that line—more than once a day—with Fiona. Teagan had taken Ailis to Keira's house today for a play day, claiming Fiona's big sister deserved a break. The two sisters were together on the bus twenty-four-seven and, given Fiona's rather overpowering presence, he thought it was a good idea to let Ailis have some time away.

"Sharing is important," he tried to stress, even though it was clear Fiona wasn't having it.

"They're my toys."

"Does Ailis share her toys with you?"

That one stumped her, but only for a minute. "Yes. I ask and she gives them to me. When she asks *me*, I say no. So that means no."

Ailis had a soft heart. No doubt she did hand her things over easily, just to keep peace.

Patrick began to understand Sky's frustration last night at dinner, so he cut his losses. "What I was trying to say is your name suits you because in this instance, fair means pretty."

"Oh!" Fiona's eyes widened. "It's my dress."

He reached out and ruffled her hair. "It's more than that."

"My mommy is pretty."

He nodded. "That she is. And while, yes, these rosy cheeks and bright eyes and red hair all make you pretty, there are some things on the inside that do the same thing as well."

"What things?"

"Your boundless energy. And how smart and funny you are. And your inner strength."

Fiona's nose crinkled. "What's that?"

"You know who you are, Fee. That's a very unusual thing, and something you rarely see in young children. You are strong. But that comes with some responsibility, you know?"

"Like what?"

Patrick thought of quiet Ailis. "You need to use your strength to help others who maybe aren't as strong see the good in themselves. Fair means pretty. And it means what your mommy says too."

"Fiona means fair," she repeated. Fiona gave him a look that said she was only buying about half of what he was selling.

He covered his mouth with his hand to hide his smile. A handful indeed.

"I like being pretty. But I'm never going to want to share." She pierced him with a look that drove home exactly how intelligent his young granddaughter was. "I want what I want," she explained. "And I want everything," she added in an adorable voice she clearly meant to be scary.

"Everything, hm? And what would that include, my fair Fiona?"

"I want to have a big house with a ballroom and a handsome prince who rubs my feet like Daddy does for Mommy. I want lots of pretty dresses and jewelry and a crown and a convertible and a cook who makes me whatever I want to eat, and I want to be famous, like Mommy and Daddy. You can come live with me if you want."

"Ah, so you *can* share."

She giggled.

"That's a very generous offer. Thank you. And what are you going to be when you grow up to be able to afford all these wonderful things…apart from a princess, of course."

Fiona smiled and never hesitated. "I'm going to tell stories."

Patrick waited for her to explain, but Fiona clearly thought that said it all.

A storyteller. He considered her nonstop narratives since their arrival in Baltimore yesterday morning. Fiona had regaled him with no less than thirty tales from the road, and he'd been enthralled by every single one.

Leave it to Fiona to have her life figured out by five.

Patrick reached over and ruffled her hair affectionately. "I think that sounds just fine. Never lose sight of that goal, Fee, and you'll be happy indeed."

Chapter One

"You sure you're doing okay?" Fiona asked again.

Padraig gave her a grin that seemed like a shadow of his former one. "I'm sure, Fee. Honest."

She nodded and took his words at face value, praying they were the truth. Padraig's beloved wife, Mia, had passed away a couple of weeks earlier. Her memorial service had been two days ago and since then, the entire family had joined forces to keep him busy, to make sure he didn't feel alone in his grief.

Fiona had only met Mia a handful of times over the year she and Padraig had been married, but she'd adored the upbeat, lovely woman.

She'd invited Padraig to join her for lunch at her family's bar, Pat's Pub. They were currently on Sunday's Side, indulging in massive cheeseburgers and fries.

"Pop Pop said you're taking some time off," she said.

Padraig nodded. "Yeah. I'm heading to Uncle Aaron's cabin on the Shenandoah River for a week. Taking Seamus for long walks in the woods and doing some fishing. Kind of looking forward to getting away."

"I suspect it'll be Seamus taking you for walks. That dog is wild."

Padraig chuckled. "Yeah. Probably should sign him up for obedience school, but I've kind of gotten used to his hijinks. Not sure I want to make him boring, well-behaved, and trained like all the other dogs in the world."

"You really want to go away? By yourself?" Fiona couldn't understand how that would be helpful. She thrived in the presence of people and hated being alone.

Padraig rearranged the fries on his plate…again. He was playing with his food more than eating it. She tried not to notice that he'd obviously lost some weight since the holidays. The new year had not been kind to him.

"I love this family, Fee, and everything everyone has done for me the past few months, but I need a break. I walk in a room and everyone stops laughing and starts talking quieter, like I can't handle happiness anymore. I don't blame anyone for that, I really don't, but I don't want everyone feeling like they have to change the way they feel and act to match me. I just had my guts ripped out. I'm the one who needs to figure out how to deal with that."

"Paddy," she started.

"Besides, I can't be in the apartment without feeling Mia's presence there. Time is the only thing that's going to help, so I'm taking some for myself. Talked to Aunt Lauren about it and she didn't see any harm in getting away for a bit, coming back and starting fresh. I like the idea of that. There's a cycle of sadness looming over us here and we need to break it."

"If you get lonely, you only have to call. I can come visit. And I know Colm and Kelli and—"

"I'm going to be fine. Promise."

She reached across the table, took his hand and squeezed it. "I'm going to hold you to that."

He grinned, and this time it felt more genuine, more like the real Padraig. "I wouldn't worry about me extending my week's vacation. Gonna have to get back in time to watch you and your friends film that show. Want my cameo."

Fiona laughed. Six months earlier, she'd arranged to have the season finale of *Wild Winters* filmed at Pat's Pub.

After graduating from college, she and her best friends, Asher, Owen and Teddy, had decided to try to shop the sitcom they'd written as a lark during their senior year at USC. Each of them had made some connections during their tenure at the university with people in the business, and one phone call led to another that led to a meeting, and before they knew it, *Wild Winters* was on the air and a weekly staple with Owen in the starring role as well as sitting at the writer's table with them. People were calling it "*Seinfeld* for Millennials" and it had taken over the number one spot halfway during its second year of production.

She was living a dream life, her days spent surrounded by her best friends, living on coffee and donuts as they laughed their asses off, trying to out-joke each other. With the show's continued success, the list of famous people who wanted cameos or even recurring bit parts had grown, and Fiona had actually walked down the red carpet the last two years, climbing the stairs with the guys to the stage to accept an Emmy for Outstanding Writing in a Comedy Series.

Pop Pop told her she lived under a lucky star, and she believed him. She was twenty-five years old and her life rocked.

It was actually Owen and Asher who'd suggested filming the season finale in Baltimore at her family's pub. They'd come up with a great gag that was tailor-made for an East Coast trip to the Irish pub. Owen's first visit to the pub had been for Thanksgiving their sophomore year in college, during the three minutes the two of them had actually dated.

Ever since, he'd always found a way to finagle an invite back, claiming he couldn't survive a year that didn't include Aunt Riley's turkey and dressing. Of course, he wasn't the only "extra" sitting around the Thanksgiving table. Once someone was unofficially adopted into the Collins family, they were in for life.

Asher had come home with her the last few summers for long weekends just to get away from the hubbub of Hollywood. He was also very quickly indoctrinated into the family, so she shouldn't have been surprised when they hit her up with the idea of filming in the pub. They loved the place as much as she did.

Her family had embraced the idea wholeheartedly and talked of nothing else since. Fiona had nearly canceled when Mia passed away, but Padraig and Pop Pop had both vetoed that decision, insisting that the show go on. She was a bit worried that was why Padraig was clearing out, hence the reason she'd asked him to lunch. If he decided having the show here would bother him, she was pulling the plug no matter what anyone else said.

"You're sure your decision to leave isn't because of the show?"

Padraig narrowed his eyes. "I'm only saying this one more time, Fiona. You have to film that show here. For one thing, it would be huge for business, and for another, it's going to give everyone else the same break I'm trying to get. I haven't been the only one hurting these past few months. I'm grateful to have you and your friends here. Filming that sitcom will give everyone something good, something fun, to focus on for a little while. They need that. They deserve that after all they've done for me."

She sighed and accepted his words. "Okay." She smiled and squeezed his hand tighter. "Okay," she repeated.

He squeezed her hand back, then released it to take a sip of his soda.

"Actually, you're probably smart to escape this week. The producer is calling for some last-minute rewrites, and setting up the cameras and doing the blocking is going to be tedious as hell. The majority of the cast isn't even showing up until the week you get back. Not to mention, I've gotta try to deal with the ultimate diva himself, Owen Winters. Ever since he won that second Emmy for Best Actor in a Comedy, he's been impossible to live with."

Padraig feigned shock. "What? Owen? A diva? No way. Playboy maybe, but diva?"

"The man is a menace."

Her cousin wasn't fooled by her words. "He's been one of your best friends since freshman year at USC. You would have dumped him seven years ago if that was really the case."

"I did dump him. Sophomore year. He's like herpes. Keeps coming back."

Padraig tilted his head and lifted one shoulder, a sure sign he was about to start teasing her. "The way Owen tells it, he dumped you."

"We dated for three minutes. That was all the time I needed to know he wasn't my type."

Padraig smiled. "In truth, Fee, I've always thought Owen *was* your type, more than that Brock guy anyway."

Fiona glanced around the restaurant. No one was nearby, so she decided to come clean. "Brock and I broke up."

"Good." It was a simple one-word answer that confirmed she was right to start breaking this news with Padraig.

Fiona giggled. "Yeah. It is."

"It was long overdue. The two of you were apart more than together, and it never sounded like your paths were headed in the same direction. Can I add that I hope you dumped *him*?"

Her grin grew. "I did. I totally did. In February."

"Man. I guess I *am* out of the loop if I'm just now hearing about it."

She shook her head. "You're not. Actually, you *are* the loop. I haven't told anyone else."

"Why not?"

Fiona shrugged. "I wanted to make sure it stuck this time."

"Will it?" Padraig asked.

She didn't hesitate to nod. "It's sticking."

"Good," Padraig repeated. "So it's time for you to find a nice guy. Owen—"

She scowled. "No way. He has an overinflated opinion of himself. Trust me when I say, no one will ever love Owen more than he loves himself."

"Me thinks she doth protest too much."

"Wow, Paddy. You're a regular poet. Come up with that all on your own?"

"Then what about your other fella? Asher. He's a nice guy."

Fiona grinned at her cousin's attempts at matchmaking. "He's very nice. But we've drifted too far over the line in our relationship. He's like a brother to me. I know too much about him and he knows *way* too much about me."

"You're protesting again."

Fiona rolled her eyes and growled.

Padraig winked at her, and they started eating again. She was delighted when he picked up his burger and actually took a big bite. Hope emerged. Padraig was going to be okay.

"Whoa, Fee. You might wanna take it easy on the grease there," Owen said, hip-bumping her over in the booth so he could sit down and grab a couple fries from her plate.

Owen was terrible at greetings, something she constantly gave him shit for. He'd come in, interrupt whatever was happening with a conversation of his own choosing, then realize several minutes in that he hadn't even said hello. They'd actually written that habit into the show as a running gag, and it always got a lot of laughs.

"Get your own," she said, tugging her plate away.

Owen ignored her and continued stealing fries.

"So you guys made it to Baltimore, huh? Asher and Teddy here?" she asked.

"Yeah. We got to the hotel about an hour ago. They're unpacking."

"Owen," Padraig said, reaching out to shake his hand. "It's good to see you again."

"Oh yeah. Hey, Paddy. You too, man. I'm fucking starving. Food on the plane was shit." Owen pushed Fiona's hands away easily, grabbing her burger and helping himself to two big bites before returning it to the plate.

She leaned back and sighed. Owen thought with three things: his dick, his stomach and then his brain, which was a distant third in the lineup. She shoved the rest of her lunch toward him. "Here. I don't want it anymore. It has your boy cooties on it."

Owen reached over her for the salt and vinegar, pouring both on the fries before digging in with gusto. And that was when the light went on and Owen realized he'd forgotten to say hello. He put the food down and focused on her cousin. "Damn. I'm sorry about that. How are you doin', P? I've been thinking about you a lot."

"I'm hanging in there."

"I was really sorry to hear about Mia. She was awesome. The best."

Padraig nodded his thanks. "She was." Then he quickly changed the subject. "Fiona tells me you have a couple busy weeks ahead of you."

Owen, bless him, took the subject switch in stride, recognizing the fact Padraig didn't want to talk about his loss. "Same shit, different coast. Going to be cool filming the finale here in the pub. Nice of your family to let us take over like this."

"Pop Pop is beside himself, really excited about it. He's been practicing that line you've given him for weeks. Starting to remind me of that old *Seinfeld* gag with all his different renditions. 'These pretzels are making me thirsty.'"

They laughed as Padraig wiped his mouth and glanced around. "Guess I better start saying my goodbyes. Want to get on the road by two, so I'm not trying to find my way to that cabin in the woods in the dark. Thanks for the company, Fee."

She nodded. "Gonna miss you. If you get bored, come back early, okay?"

"I'll be home in one week, ready to wow those cameras of yours with my bartending skills."

They all stood, Padraig giving her a hug then shaking Owen's hand again. He headed toward the kitchen, starting his farewells with Riley.

Fiona studied Owen's appearance, aware that he'd done well to hide his identity on the walk from the hotel to the pub. Owen preferred the hipster look, and he was working it today. With his beard, knit cap, and colorful tats peeking out beneath the short sleeves of his dark gray T-shirt, strangers would probably pass him on the street assuming he was a musician in a grunge band, until they took a harder look and realized he was a TV star.

She sat back down and Owen followed her in, reclaiming the same spot. She pointed across the booth. "Other side is free now."

He leaned back, resting his arm along the bench seat, ignoring her. "Feels good to be back." Owen glanced around the restaurant. "Forgot how pretty the girls are in Baltimore. And on this coast, my fame and good looks seems more potent, you know what I mean? Less competition once I'm out of Hollywood."

"Is that the real reason you suggested filming in Baltimore? So you could hold the monopoly on TV star?"

He gave her a wink that was annoyingly charming, even though his words aggravated the shit out of her. "I like getting laid. It's going to be a busy month."

Sometimes she wondered why she hung out with Owen. When he started strutting and bragging about his fame or his sexual conquests, she was hard-pressed not to throat punch him.

"We're here to work, remember?"

Owen turned to face her, and Fiona was forced to admit why his flirty nature never truly bothered her. He really was hot. And funny. And while he pretended to be a ladies' man, she suspected a lot of that was more bluster than truth.

"Work *is* play, you know that."

"I'm surprised you're okay with this trip. Thought you were in love with…what's-her-name?"

He chuckled. "Ashley Four. It's over. She was a stage-ten clinger."

Fiona rolled her eyes. "Of course. How could I forget that name?" She and the other guys had taken to numbering his girlfriends with the same names in an attempt to distinguish who exactly they were talking about. So far, they'd had to tabulate up to four Ashleys, three Brittanys and two Amandas. "Do me a favor. Next time you meet an Ashley, walk away. It hasn't been a good name for you."

"I'll keep that in mind, but I'm not making any promises. If she's got nice tits, I'm going for five."

"You're a pig."

He laughed. "You know I'm just trying to get a rise out of you. Why don't we text Teddy and Asher and tell them to bring their laptops and we'll work from here? Figure we can knock out the changes Al wanted better if we're in the pub."

Fiona made a buzzer noise to indicate he'd given the wrong answer. "Errrr. No. No work will happen in the pub because you'll start ordering pitchers, gossiping about Hollywood stars with Pop Pop and his cronies, and we'll all be three sheets to the wind before dusk."

As always, Owen ignored her and sent off the text. Teddy replied instantly that they would be there in five. Owen, Teddy and Asher were sharing a suite at a hotel just around the corner.

Fiona had opted for staying at the Collins Dorm above the pub while she was home, sleeping in Caitlyn and Ailis's old room. It had been dubbed the Collins Dorm by Aunt Riley when the grandkids began moving into the spacious apartment where their parents had lived with Pop Pop while growing up.

Unlike most of her cousins, Fiona had never lived in Baltimore, her childhood spent on a tour bus with her parents and Ailis. Fiona had always loved life on the move, a different city every night, while Ailis had been less fond of it.

The second Ailis graduated from high school, she'd set up camp in Baltimore, determined to make up for every second of the time she'd lost with the family while growing up. That decision lasted only a few years until her homebody sister fell in love with someone just like their dear old dad, Sky Mitchell. Which meant Ailis was back on the road, on another tour bus, with Hunter Maxwell. Hunter's star was on the rise, and Fiona couldn't be happier for him. The guy was seriously talented, but more than that, he was just as head over heels for Ailis as her sister was for him. They fit together perfectly, and for the first time in her life, Fiona actually felt a bit jealous of her quiet, responsible, dependable, sensible sister.

Her oldest cousin, Caitlyn, had also moved out of the dorm, opting to live with her uber-hot billionaire boyfriend, Lucas Whiting, which meant there was an empty bedroom in the apartment for her to use.

Fiona had never felt the need to live near the family and was cool with just visiting from time to time. Baltimore was freaking cold in the winter, and after four years of college in sunny California, she'd discovered she was made for heat, not snow.

But that didn't mean she didn't sometimes regret missing out on so much. Her family was, hands down, the greatest, craziest, most fun crew in the world, and there'd been too many Facetime conversations where she'd found herself jealous not to be in the same room.

She was in Baltimore for a month, and Fiona intended to take advantage of that time, to immerse herself in a true Collins lifestyle.

Her cousin Yvonne came over to clear their table. "Hey, Owen, when did you get here?"

"Just a few minutes ago. Good to see you again, Yvonne."

"Did you want to order anything?" she asked.

The asshole rubbed his full stomach, claiming he couldn't eat another bite. Fiona decided hitting the pub side probably wasn't such a bad thing. She was still hungry and in the mood for Aunt Riley's spicy shrimp appetizer. God, Owen wasn't wrong. Too long in Baltimore, around all this good cooking, and she was destined to gain fifty pounds. She'd have to take Yvonne up on her invitation to go running in the morning with her and her BFF, Leo.

"We're heading over to the pub side, waiting for the other guys so we can do some work," Owen said, rising from the booth and reaching down to help her out. Fiona gave him a funny look, not used to his chivalry. Then she decided he was probably putting on a show for Yvonne. The guy was a master at charming women. Except her, of course. For one thing, she wasn't fooled by his act, and for another, Owen had put her firmly in the one-of-the-guys category years ago. Right after their breakup in college.

"Cool," Yvonne said. "Uncle Tris is working. He can set you up with drinks. I'll stop by once the other two get here and see if they want some food."

Owen gave Yvonne a smile and a wink and then they headed for a corner booth in the pub. Uncle Tris waved to indicate he'd seen them and would be over in a minute. The bar was relatively quiet right now, but Fiona knew that would change as soon as five o'clock hit and folks started heading in for their happy hours.

They hadn't been there a full minute before Teddy and Asher walked in, looking around. Owen gave them a wave. He'd claimed the seat next to her again, but she didn't bother to mention it since she knew the other guys were coming.

Asher slid in first, sitting across from her, and Teddy followed. She grinned as she watched both men do exactly what she expected. Asher pulled his laptop from the case, firing it up, clearly ready to get straight to work.

Meanwhile, Teddy's eyes had yet to land on anyone at the table. He was doing his usual scan of the room in search of available guys.

"Slim pickings," he murmured before catching a glimpse of Tris behind the bar. "Well hello, mountain man. I wouldn't mind taking a drink from your tap, Daddy."

Fiona crinkled her nose. "Um…gross. That's my uncle Tris, Teddy. He's very married and very straight."

Teddy sighed. "That's a loss for our side. No worries though. I've been exploring Tinder, and while the Beach Boys might long for California girls, I'm not going to lie, Maryland has some very fine boys."

Asher pushed his glasses up on his nose, tsking quietly. He was the hottest nerd on the planet, something Fiona liked to tease him about. He was Clark Kent incarnate with his dark clean-cut hairstyle and black-rimmed glasses that did nothing to hide his ice-blue eyes, only serving to accentuate his strong jawline.

Fiona sighed. She really needed to stop looking at her best friends so closely. It did nothing to improve her current dateless, sexless, horny state.

"We're only here a few weeks, Teddy. Isn't it wrong to try to find someone on Tinder when you're not planning on sticking around? You'd be leading them on."

Teddy wrapped his arm around Asher's shoulders in a friendly manner, even as his face revealed something more like pity. "I always forget how young and innocent you are, my son. There's this little thing called a hookup, Ash. It's all about the three F's. Foreplay, forward thrusting and farewell. The only man with whom I'd ever consider exploring the fourth F—forever—is you, and you refuse to come out of the closet."

Owen and Fiona both laughed as Asher closed his eyes in his typical praying-for-patience style. "I've told you a million times, Ted. I'm not gay."

Teddy shrugged his shoulders as if the words meant nothing. This joke was nothing new. In fact, in their little foursome of comedy writers, they probably shared no less than a hundred inside jokes, and this one was the oldest.

Funny how it never really got old.

Teddy wiggled his eyebrows. "Come on, Ash. Come to the dark side. It's fun over here. We have lightsabers."

Asher, their eternal straight man—literally and figuratively—shook his head. "You, me and Owen have been roommates since freshman year of college. I've seen both of your lightsabers a thousand times. Believe me, neither has tempted me to give up Princess Leia's buns."

"Hey," Owen said, "why you gotta drag me into this? My lightsaber is pretty spectacular. Tell him, Fee."

She shook her head. "You know the rule. When it turns to *Star Wars* puns, I'm out."

None of the men had a chance to complain.

"That reminds me." Asher handed something across the table to Fiona.

"What's this?" she asked—then she recognized the material. "My sweater."

"You mentioned on the phone it was chillier in Baltimore than you'd expected, so I swung by your place to get it."

Fiona smiled, touched by the sweet gesture. "That was so nice of you."

Asher shrugged off the compliment, looking somewhat relieved to have her grateful attention distracted from him when Tris arrived.

"Hey, Fiona, fellas." He looked at Teddy, and Fiona did the introductions, as he was the only one of her friends who hadn't been to the pub before.

"Uncle Tris, this is Teddy Martin, the other writer on the show. And you remember Owen Winters and Asher McCarthy, of course."

Tris shook all their hands. "Sure do." He gestured behind the bar to the framed, signed headshot Owen had given Tris during his last visit. "Still appreciate the picture, Owen. You got a lot of fans on this side of the country. They're always impressed when they hear my niece writes for *Wild Winters* and find out you've been in the bar before."

Owen preened. The guy loved being famous. Way too much. "Yeah, well, I feel there's something I should confess, Tris. It's been weighing heavy on my mind for quite a while now, and I think I need to come clean."

Fiona leaned back and resisted the urge to roll her eyes. Owen was about to launch into some big old pile of ridiculousness, judging by his dramatic tone. The man truly was born to be an actor.

"Oh yeah?" Tris asked with a slight grin.

"As you know, the first time I was here, Fee and I were only nineteen and on break from college. I was young and in love—"

Teddy pretended to cough, barking out the word "lust" as he did so.

Tris snickered.

Owen continued as if nothing had happened. "I was an innocent boy, really, and I'm afraid I was led astray. Fiona insisted that we sneak down here in the middle of the night and steal a few shots of whiskey." He gestured toward her. "There wasn't anything I wouldn't do to impress her and, well…she made me do it. I told her it was wrong, but she wouldn't listen."

Fiona recalled that night very well. And everything he said was true. But the roles were reversed.

Tris laughed. "Yeah. That's our Fee. Bad to the bone."

She snorted at her uncle's joke.

"Just the same," Tris said, "I'll be sure to add those drinks to your tab tonight in order to help clear that conscience of yours, Owen."

Owen frowned. "But—"

"No, no," Tris said, well able to give as good as he got. "No more apologies. Nothing like cold hard cash to absolve you of your sins."

"You sure he's straight?" Teddy asked Fiona, not bothering to hide his question from Tris. "No shot he's even a little gay?"

"No shot," Tris replied. "But my wife is stopping by later if you want to consult with her on that."

Teddy gave him a wink. "Well, if you ever change your mind…"

"You'll be the first man I call." Tris laughed. "What'll you have?"

"Pitcher?" Owen said, looking around the table.

"Yeah," Asher said. "We start drinking liquor and no work will get done. What's that beer Baltimore is famous for?"

Fiona winced. "No. Hell no. For the love of all that's holy, can we drink something other than Natty Boh?"

"How about Guinness then?" Teddy asked as he wiggled his eyebrows at Tris. "As a nod to our charming Irish host."

Fiona tried to hide her smile behind her hand at Teddy's over-the-top flirting with her fifty-something uncle.

Tris grinned and shook his head. "I can tell you're going to be trouble. We're going to have a talk later, Fee, about the company you're keeping in California."

"Sounds long overdue, Uncle Tris."

Tris returned to the bar and Asher tried to get them on track. "Okay. Let me just pull up the file of the script. Here it is. 'Anything Goes.'"

The finale was going to be a wild ride for the show as the main characters decide to spend one night in "anything goes" mode while on an impromptu trip to Baltimore. The concept had been Fiona's, and they'd all fallen in love with the idea that for one night, all the characters would do whatever they wanted without fear of consequences…and with hilarious results, of course. It was Fiona's favorite script so far, and she couldn't wait to see the finished product.

Though she didn't tell him often, lest it gave him an even bigger head, Owen was probably one of the best comedic actors she'd ever seen. Actually, the whole ensemble was over-the-top talented. It was one of the reasons the show was such a hit. *Entertainment Weekly* had run an article just a few weeks ago, claiming that *Wild Winters* had found the award-winning combination of writing and acting with Owen Winters at the helm.

They'd given him some serious shit for that quote, though Owen swore up one side and down the other he'd never told the reporter he was in charge. Fiona tended to believe that was the truth. While they liked to call their work a team effort, there was no denying

Asher was the one they'd all point to if anyone asked who the lead writer was, and she would probably be a close second.

The rest of the cast was arriving in a week for the filming, which meant Asher was right. They really did need to buckle down and get to work. The producer had asked for quite a few changes, and a couple of them were pretty massive.

Asher continued clicking keys. "Let me open my email. Al sent a list of things he wants changed, including that part in the opening scene where—"

Teddy's phone pinged and his eyes lit up. "Ooo la la. My night just got interesting."

Asher peered over, squinting at the picture. "Who is that?"

"Dimitur. My little Bulgarian bonbon. Tinder has been very, very good to me."

"That can't be a real guy," Asher persisted. "He looks like a model. Twenty bucks says someone is trying to catfish you."

"Let me see," Owen said, grabbing the phone from Teddy. "Damn. If his lightsaber matches the rest of him…"

Fiona snuck a peek, her eyes widening. "Whoa. That's a loss for *our* team…if he's real."

Teddy scowled. "Of course he's real."

"Just the same, plan to meet him here. You can grab a table in the pub and we can keep an eye on you." Poor Asher had been the dad of their group since they were eighteen years old.

"Fine. Oh! He wants to FaceTime. I'm going outside."

Teddy was gone within seconds, passing Tris, who was on the way to their table with their pitcher and mugs.

"That Teddy guy is a piece of work," Tris said with a chuckle. "Pop is going to love him."

"My fear is he'll flirt with Pop Pop too."

Tris laughed at Fiona's genuine concern. "Oh my God. I'd pay to see that. Enjoy the beer. I'll be back to check on you in a little while."

Owen grinned and waved to two women at a nearby table who'd obviously recognized him.

Asher looked longingly at his computer. "I told Teddy coming here to work was a mistake."

"I said the same thing." Fiona looked away when the two women started giggling, daring each other to come over and say hi. Sometimes she was really embarrassed by her gender.

"Owen." She waved her hand in front of his face.

He misunderstood her annoyance, picking up the pitcher and pouring her a glass. "Oh, sorry, Fee."

"I'm not worried about the beer. I thought we were going to try to work on this scene."

Owen had already turned his attention back to the women at the other table.

Asher closed the lid on his laptop. "This is pointless." He picked up his beer and took a long drink. "I love Guinness. What do you say we get shitfaced tonight and hit the ground running tomorrow?"

Chapter Two

"Finally. Asher for the win. I'm all-in on shitfaced," Owen said, raising his glass as well, chugging the dark lager.

Fiona had been around these guys long enough to know that resistance was futile, and if she was really being honest, she didn't feel like working anyway.

One pitcher turned to two, then three, then the happy-hour crowd started rolling in. Her uncles Killian and Justin stopped by their table to say hello as they waited for their wife, Lily, to join them after she got off work at the Baltimore aquarium. They were indulging in their weekly Sweet Thursday tradition, which Uncle Killian explained was their way of getting a jump on the weekend, a pregame happy hour to kick off Friday and Saturday with style. They went to grab a table, their usual from the looks of it, and ordered their own pitcher of Guinness.

She glanced around the room, delighted to be in the midst of so many members of her family. This didn't happen often, so when it did, she made sure she enjoyed it.

Tris and Padraig loved live music, so whenever they could get someone to play at the bar, they did. The

Thursday-night crowd was being treated to some classic covers by a local band.

Fiona took another sip of beer, then giggled at something Asher said, the Guinness working its way through her until she felt boneless and carefree. Teddy's bonbon arrived shortly after six, and the two of them grabbed a table in a quiet corner. The guy was real—and he was even better looking in person.

"Maybe I should check out Tinder," she murmured.

Her words captured both Asher's and Owen's attention, and she realized the beer had loosened her tongue.

"Wouldn't that piss Brock off?" Owen asked. Her best friends had just sort of begrudgingly accepted her boyfriend. Which meant she was about to make both of them very happy.

"We broke up."

Owen's eyes narrowed suspiciously, and Asher was even slower to believe. "When?"

She bit her lip. "Six weeks ago."

"What?" Owen asked loudly, drawing attention from several nearby tables. "Why are we just now hearing about this?"

She crinkled her nose. "Because it was kind of a dick move on my part."

Asher smiled. "What did you do?"

"Dumped him on Valentine's Day," she mumbled.

Owen's brows creased, clearly confused. "Didn't he send you a dozen long stems on Valentine's? You got them at the office and all the women acted like he'd sent you a million bucks or something."

She nodded. "Yeah. He sent flowers."

"Wow," Asher said. "That *is* a dick move."

Owen shook his head. "I'm not buying it. Not buying that as your reason for not telling us about the breakup. It's been six weeks, Fee. You've had plenty of opportunities to say something. Why didn't you?"

She needed new friends. Ones who didn't know her so well. She never got away with a damn thing with these guys. "I was afraid I'd backslide."

Asher sighed. "The big gesture."

She nodded, then instantly revised her opinion. In truth, there was something very comforting and safe in being able to say absolutely anything without fear of judgment. Owen, Asher and Teddy loved her, warts and all.

"He didn't really send those roses. The card was signed 'Love, Brock'…in his secretary's handwriting."

Owen grinned. "Much as it pains me to say this, you should probably cut him some slack. The guy *is* in Dubai, Fee."

Brock Vanderbilt was a talented civil engineer, and it wasn't unusual for his job to take him out of the state or the country for several months at a time. However, the old adage that absence makes the heart fonder never seemed to apply to her and Brock. They were as tumultuous on different continents as they were in the same city.

The man was her white whale, her Kryptonite. She'd started dating him a few months after she and Owen split in college and over the past five years, they'd engaged in a never-ending cycle of on-again, off-again. Teddy joked after their last split that they'd just broken Ross and Rachel's record on *Friends*. At least, she thought it was a joke. Sadly, as a comedy writer, she knew every joke held a kernel of truth.

The problem was, Brock was a master of big gestures. She'd break things off, then he'd swoop back on the scene with some over-the-top, killer romantic gesture and, like a sucker, she'd fall for it, hook, line and Cyndi Lauper-style. Time after time.

"I know he's in Dubai. It's just…God, I keep trying to make him something he's not."

"He's not your dad."

This wasn't a new conversation. "I know, Asher. My father adores my mom and they love spending time together—even if it's doing something as simple as watching a movie on the couch with microwave popcorn. I mean, he seriously loves her, would die for her, and he wants to be with her. Is it so wrong to want the same thing? To want to be the center of someone's universe? To matter to someone on that level?"

Asher chuckled. "Admit it. You want to be the center of *everyone's* universe, Fee."

"Oh, shut up. I do not." Then, because she could never lie to them, she added, "Not much, anyway."

Owen wrapped his arm around her shoulders and tugged her close. "You can be the center of mine. And Asher's and Teddy's."

She pulled away from his friendly embrace, her eyes narrowed. "You mean I'm not already?"

Owen picked up his beer. "Stuck my foot in it there. So what makes you think the breakup is going to stick this time?"

"I told you. It's been six weeks. All my previous backslides all occurred within two weeks of the split."

"Which would be impressive—if Brock were in the country. But it's easy to swear off a guy who's on another continent. What happens when he reappears in California and stands outside your bedroom window with a boom box over his head like fucking John Cusack?" Owen asked.

"Oooo…*Say Anything*," she murmured. "That *would* be hot. And hard to resist." She, Asher, Teddy and Owen had a standing monthly date where they ate pepperoni pizza, drank cheap beer and watched cheesy eighties movies. It was hands down Fiona's favorite night of every month. Last month's fare had been *Doc Hollywood.* A dashing, young Michael J. Fox in the '80s. Her kind of man.

"Seriously, Fiona," Asher said. "You have to admit your record when it comes to Brock isn't stellar. What makes this any different from the last twenty-two breakups?"

And this was why she hadn't told the guys about dumping Brock. Because she did have a shitty track record. And even though, deep down in her heart, she knew it was over, there was nothing short of time that was going to prove her sincerity to her best friends.

"There have only been eight legit breakups," she said, in a weak-hearted attempt to defend herself.

"And forty-seven minor skirmishes," Asher added to tease her.

"Listen, I get it. I know I've been the queen of backsliding when it comes to Brock, and me just saying it's different this time doesn't really hold a lot of weight, but—"

"Why do you think it's different this time?" Leave it to Asher to give her a chance. While Owen was clearly still skeptical, Asher would always believe. It was what she loved about both of them. One kept her grounded while the other let her dream.

"I got those roses, saw the card, and realized we were both just going through the motions. I didn't get excited by the flowers. They didn't spark any romantic feelings. In fact, they sort of pissed me off. Because I knew he'd sent them out of some sense of obligation *after* his secretary reminded him it was Valentine's Day. When he's away, he's not thinking about me. And that was when I realized…I'm never thinking about *him*, either. When he's around, we serve as eye candy for the other's work functions, we go out to fancy restaurants, and he drags me to that stuffy country club he belongs to, where I pretend to enjoy spending time with all the snooty doctors' wives while he talks golf, drinks whiskey and smokes cigars."

"You don't like those women?" Owen asked, feigning shock. If there was one thing they could rely on, it was Fiona's head exploding after a night at *the club*. "And here I was thinking you were going to start training for the next marathon with them."

"If I ever say 'Oh, wouldn't running twenty-six miles be a fun way to spend a Saturday?' shoot me. You know the rule…"

"You only run that far if someone is chasing you with a knife," Asher and Owen said in unison.

"Right. I jog every morning just so I can eat more fries and drink more wine. My running has a purpose."

Asher put the conversation back on track. "I hate to be *that* guy, but none of these Brock complaints are exactly news, Fee."

"I know. I'm sitting here pointing out all the bad stuff because I have to keep justifying to myself that I made the right decision. I called him when I got home on Valentine's to say thanks and before I knew it, the words were sort of spilling out of me. I asked him if he loved me, and he said he did, but there was this tone in his voice…"

Owen sighed. "Are you sure you heard a tone?"

Fiona was big on tone. It was sort of her thing. And it drove the guys nuts. "Yes. He sounded tired. Like he was only saying he loved me because he had to."

"That's not a good tone."

She looked at Owen, trying to decide if he was teasing her. When he didn't crack a smile, she forged on. "I don't love him anymore. I knew it on Valentine's Day. I'm not sure I didn't know it back in the summer when we split up the seventh time for those three days. I have to stop trying so hard to make him the one. He's a nice guy, with a great job. And yes, he's attractive, and sex with him was decent, but—"

"If a woman ever said sex with me was just 'decent,' I'd jump off a bridge. That's not exactly high praise," Asher muttered.

Fiona grinned, then finished her thought. "He doesn't make my heart race anymore."

"Okay," Asher said quietly after studying her face a few moments, and she knew that she'd convinced him. Owen still looked dubious, but she'd prove it to him eventually. For now, she was glad to have come clean with them.

"Hey," Teddy said, sitting back down at the booth. "Bonbon is in the bathroom. Thoughts?"

"He's sex-on-a-stick fine," Fiona said.

Teddy's eyes lit up. "Right? Not bad to look at…*aaaaaat allllllll*." He drew out the last two words. "It's a shame he's eleven eggs short of a dozen. What are you talking about over here? Looked serious for a second."

Asher nodded his head toward her. "Fiona broke up with Brock on Valentine's Day."

Teddy's expression didn't change a bit. "When does he get back from Dubai?"

"May," she said.

"Yeah. Right. Let's revisit this conversation then. So, listen, about the sleeping arrangements in the hotel suite. There are two rooms, one with a king and the other with two queens. I'm thinking, since neither one of *you* are probably going to hook up tonight, that I should get my own room."

Fiona looked at Owen. "I'm not the center of Teddy's universe."

He laughed. "Are you sure you want to be?"

Teddy snapped his fingers. "Focus, people. Bonbon. Boom-boom." He glanced over at the table he just left.

"Shit. He's back. So we're good on the room situation?"

Asher nodded. "We're good."

Teddy was gone within seconds.

Fiona watched as Teddy led his Tinder true love to the dance floor for an extremely provocative bump and grind. "I wish I was a gay guy."

"If you were, Asher would never be able to hit on you. Since he's super straight," Owen joked.

She grinned, then glanced at her phone. "You know, maybe it wouldn't be such a bad thing to check out some of those dating sites. I could try it while we're here. Just as a test run, since I have my escape route back to the West Coast all lined up."

Asher shook his head. "No. You and I are making a pact right now. No online-dating desperation."

She leaned back and huffed. "Dammit, Ash. I'm not making that deal. I'm having a hard time finding a decent guy on my own. Teddy swipes right three times and boom, he's getting lucky."

"Have you seriously been looking around?" Owen asked.

She nodded. "Yeah. Kind of, but nothing's clicking. I guess my wickedly good looks and brilliant mind just aren't enough anymore. Dating sites might be my last hope."

Owen laughed, reaching over to ruffle her hair—something he knew she hated—and she batted his hand away. "And you call *me* cocky."

"I'm just saying…it's been a long, cold winter and," she gestured downward with a small pout, "Happy Clam is sad."

"You know I hate it when you refer to your vagina as Happy Clam," Asher said.

She rolled her eyes. "But it's perfectly fine for you guys to call your dicks lightsabers."

Owen stretched his legs, putting his feet on the bench seat Teddy left vacant. "Tinder isn't the way to go."

She scowled. "Says the TV star who can pick up a woman three steps outside his front door on any given day of the week."

"Please refer to Teddy's previous explanation of the difference. Hookup. I haven't dated anyone I'd consider a long-term relationship with. And sometimes sleeping with groupies is worse than not dating at all."

"Seriously?" Fiona said. "You're bitching about getting laid? Who are you and where is Owen Winters?"

Owen grimaced and didn't bother to argue his point any further.

Asher shrugged. "I'm siding with Fee on this one."

She figured he would. Asher was only one month ahead of her in the newly alone stage. He and his longtime girlfriend, Christina, had split on New Year's Eve—initiated by Asher and also a dick move, as they'd pointed out to him.

He fiddled with his mug. "At least you're getting out and doing stuff, Owen. Apart from pizza-and-beer nights with you guys, my hand is getting quite a workout."

Fiona nodded. "I had to replace the batteries on my old vibrator twice in the last year. Broke down a month ago and bought myself the Cadillac of vibrators in hopes of longevity."

"Jesus," Owen said. "Tell me again why we broke up?"

She punched him lightly on the arm, sorry he'd reminded her about their time together. Usually, she tried to forget that, tried to forget how sweet it had been with him. For all his playboy swagger, Owen had been a really considerate lover back in college. The guy had stamina, and when he went down, he stayed down until she went up and over. She'd dated too many guys who'd given Happy Clam the token swipe, then acted like it was *her* fault if she hadn't come in eight seconds. She wasn't a goddamn bull rider. A good orgasm took time.

Like Asher, most of her nights were quiet and lonely. She and the guys were together all day at work, so it wasn't like she could expect them to entertain her at night too. They limited their after-hours interaction to a night or two a week and then the occasional weekend party, depending on what was happening in Hollywood. Lately, Fiona lived for those "extra" times.

She was young, so this should be the time she was out, sowing her wild oats, partying until she dropped. She'd fucked up, committing to Brock when she was still in college. She had squandered a lot of good years.

Then she'd talk to Ailis on the phone, hear her gush about Hunter, and realize she'd rather reap the damn grain and grow old with someone than play the field. She had tried to fool herself for years that person was Brock. Now she was back at square one with precious little dating experience under her belt.

"I think I want to get married," she announced, not sure why she would say something so stupid out loud.

Owen turned his attention back to her as Asher said, "To who?"

She shrugged. "I don't know. Somebody."

Owen chuckled. "That's a solid plan, Fee. I like it. You should run with that."

"Smart-ass. I'm just saying hookups might be fine for you and Teddy, but I don't want to do that."

Owen shrugged one shoulder. "Not sure you have much of a choice. That's called single life."

"Single." She hadn't really attached that word to her name, which was ridiculous since that's what she'd been for six weeks. She perked up. "Hey, you know what? I *am* single." Her breakups with Brock in the past had been too short and halfhearted for her to ever really manage to change the Facebook status. Then something else occurred to her. "I think this is the first time in history that all four of us have been single at the same time."

Asher considered that. "You're right."

Owen slapped the table excitedly. "We should have a swingin' singles party."

If Fiona was known for her tone-reading abilities, Owen was famous for finding reasons to party. She swore the guy celebrated something almost daily, be it winning an Emmy all the way to no cavities at the dentist. He was an expert celebrator.

However, this time, Fiona was all-in. "I agree. I'll get my cousins on board. Saturday night. Big bash upstairs."

"I like it. And you realize it's April Fools' Day on Saturday, right? Sort of screams theme party." Owen lifted his glass and took a long swig of beer.

And that was when Fiona knew exactly what the theme should be. "You're right. But not swingin' singles. That's too nineteen-seventy."

Owen frowned. "I like that theme."

She shook her head, knowing he'd like hers better. "Nope. We're hosting an Anything Goes Night."

Owen's eyes widened. "Oh yeah."

"Hey. That's perfect," Asher said with a grin. "A test drive of the finale. That has the potential to help with some of the plot holes Al pointed out."

Owen groaned. "It's a party, Ash. Not work. Repeat after me. *Not work*."

Asher grinned but refused to say the words.

"Owen is right. Here's to celebrating our singleness…with raucous, improper and immature behavior," Fiona said as a toast.

Owen laughed. "My kind of party."

She, Asher and Owen tapped their glasses, draining them in an unspoken chugging contest, and then they ordered another pitcher.

Shit just got real.

Chapter Three

Tris had just brought them all another round when Sunnie stopped by the table.

"Hey, guys. Welcome back to Baltimore."

He and Owen both stood up to give her quick hugs. Asher was crazy about Fiona's family. There were approximately four thousand members of the Collins clan, and every single one of them was top notch. Funny, friendly, welcoming. Owen remarked once that all the Collins girls were pretty and the guys were great to drink with. The perfect genetic strand flowed from generation to generation.

"Sunnie," Fiona started, "the guys and I were just planning a big party for Saturday night. It's the first time we've all been single at the same time since freshman year of college. We want to kick up our heels."

Sunnie nodded as Fiona talked. "Sounds awesome." She reached into her back pocket and pulled out her phone.

Fiona kept describing their plans, even though Sunnie's attention was glued to her cell. "We're calling it 'Anything Goes' night, mimicking the finale we're going to tape here next week."

"Mmmhmm," Sunnie hummed.

Asher expected Fiona to stop talking, since it was clear Sunnie was more interested in texting than the conversation.

"We were thinking of holding it in the Collins Dorm," Fiona continued. "Maybe an eight o'clock start time."

"Sounds cool," Sunnie said, even though she hadn't looked up once, her thumbs gliding along the screen of her phone. Finally, she hit send. "Okay. Done."

"Awesome," Fiona said.

"What's done?" Asher asked.

Fiona's phone pinged, and she grinned at the screen as Sunnie explained. "I just sent out the invites. We have a cousin text group. I sent them the details and told them it was up to them to—"

Asher's and Owen's phones pinged almost in unison.

Sunnie laughed as Fiona held her phone up to show them the text was from her, then finished her explanation. "It's up to them to forward the invite to whoever they want to come."

"Woohoo!" Teddy yelled out from across the bar. He waved his phone as they all looked in his direction. "Parrrrrtaaaaaaay!"

Sunnie glanced back down at her phone. "Already got four yeses. This is going to be epic! I'm going to head to the kitchen and get Mom to help plan the menu. You guys are in charge of the alcohol." She pointed her finger at them. "And take it seriously. Liquor matters."

She walked toward Sunday's Side to find her mother, Riley, before any of them could reply.

Asher gave Owen a "WTF" look, but his friend didn't seem a bit fazed by anything that had just happened.

"Might be the most profound thing anyone has ever said to me," Owen mused. "Liquor matters."

Fiona was on her phone, tapping out a list. "She's not wrong. I have a pretty good idea of what everyone likes, and let's face it, it's hard to fuck up too bad when the party is happening one floor up from a bar. If we forget something or run out, we'll steal it from here."

"Fiona," Asher started, but she was laughing.

"Okay, Ash. We'll keep a list of what we take and get Uncle Tris to add it to Owen's tab. Damn," she said, putting down her phone. "Too much beer. Let me out, Owen. I have to pee."

He stood up and she slid out. When Owen resumed his seat, he wasted no time starting the conversation Asher had known was coming the second Fiona had said she'd ditched Brock.

"So," Owen began. "Fee is a free agent. You going to ask her out?"

Asher shook his head.

Owen rolled his eyes. "Let me rephrase. You *wanna* ask her out?"

Again, he didn't hesitate in his answer. It wasn't necessary. Both of Owen's questions were rhetorical because his best friend knew the answers, so Asher nodded.

"But you're not going to?"

Owen had caught Asher looking at Fiona a few weeks ago with way too much heat, too much desire, and he'd called him out for it when they were alone. Asher had stupidly said he wanted her, but it wasn't meant to be. He leaned back in the booth. "Are *you* going to ask her out?"

Owen looked away, pretending to study the people around them. "No. I had my shot with her back when we were nineteen. It didn't work out."

Asher snorted. "You were both young, inexperienced kids, prone to drama. I'd hardly call that a true shot."

"And now we're young, experienced adults, prone to drama. How is that better?"

Asher grinned. "Good point." Then he sobered up. "But you want another shot, don't you?"

Owen shrugged, clearly reluctant to show his hand. "I don't know."

Asher had fallen madly in love with Fiona Adams when they were eighteen years old. He'd always been quiet, more reserved than the rest of their gang, and he'd suffered from a fair amount of shyness back then. Their entire freshman year had passed before he could talk to Fiona without his palms sweating.

Of course, by the time he'd overcome his nervousness enough to ask her out, Owen had beat him to the punch. The eight and a half weeks Owen and Fiona had dated had been the longest of his young life.

Then Owen and Fiona had gotten into some stupid fight, something only teenagers could hype into a disaster, and had split up. Owen hadn't recovered easily. He'd gotten drunker than Asher had ever seen him the last semester of senior year and had sworn Fiona was the only girl he'd ever love. The pure pain on his best friend's face was something Asher would never forget.

Fiona had found Brock Vanderbilt within weeks of her breakup with Owen. All-American boy who'd been quarterback of his high school football team and who strutted around campus like Adonis with his frat brothers.

Fiona had been devastated the first time Brock dumped her. It was shortly after graduation, and he'd gotten a job on the East Coast. She'd actually offered to move to New York with him, but the bastard had told her they should probably take a break, get their careers settled and then decide the next step.

At that time, Asher was dating Christina, who'd been their Creative Writing professor senior year. Ten years older than him, Christina had exposed Asher to fine wine, jazz music, classical literature and kinky sex. It had ended when he realized they were trapped in their teacher-student roles and it began to chafe.

Never prone to fits of anger or passion, Christina had simply accepted that he'd outgrown her. Two weeks later, she was dating another student in her class. It was a testament to how disengaged he'd been in the relationship when he'd heard that rumor and was actually happy for her…and a little bit concerned for her next young protégé.

Fiona's first Brock split ended when the stupid man regretted his decision and showed up only a month later, and two seconds after they'd sold *Wild Winters* to the network. He whisked her away for Big Gesture Number One, a romantic weekend in Paris to celebrate.

Asher could sort of understand why she stayed with Brock. She hadn't lied. Much as he hated to admit it, Brock was a pretty stand-up guy—smart and good-looking. Asher figured most of his and Owen's problem with the man stemmed from the fact that he didn't have much of a sense of humor. He laughed at all the right times, but there was something in the sound that always made Asher think he either didn't get the joke or didn't find it funny. Both were cardinal sins in his mind.

"We're a couple of idiots," Owen said, still not looking his direction, his gaze fixed on Teddy and his date holding hands at their table. Romance always came easy to Teddy.

"I guess we are. It was easier to go about life as usual when she was dating Brock. Now that she's free…" Asher didn't finish his sentence, because it was clear Owen knew what he was thinking. As long as Fiona dated Brock, all was well because they didn't have to think about the fact they were both in love with the same girl.

Teddy popped back over. "Hey. What gives with the gloomy faces?"

"Nothing," Owen said, his tone a dead giveaway.

Teddy groaned. "Jesus Christ. The Free Fiona pining has already started?"

Asher shrugged, not wanting to admit his friend had hit the nail in one, but something else was bothering him more. "How did you know—"

"Jesus, Ash. You're as transparent as glass," Teddy interrupted. "I mean, you were distracted during the Christina years, but in college and ever since New Year's, you can't *look* at Fee without getting a boner. Pretty sure you've moved the writing table at work forward with that monster six inches since January."

Asher grimaced, hating how easy he was to read, so he deflected. "Owen's pouting too."

Teddy looked at Owen and scowled, but Owen didn't take the bait, didn't bother to defend himself.

Finally, Teddy threw his hands in the air. "No," he said loudly. "We're not doing this. Do yourselves a favor. Look around at all the available ladies. Find a pretty one you like and ask her to dance. Then invite her back to the hotel and screw out some of this pent-up lust—but not in the room with the king-size bed. I dibbsed that first. If you don't use your dicks enough, they wither up and fall off. It's a scientifically proven fact."

"We'll take it under advisement," Asher said with a chuckle. Thank God for Teddy. The man always knew how to make him laugh.

Owen rubbed his chin, glancing around the bar. "He makes a good point. We both know how this is going to end, and when."

"May. Big gesture," Asher muttered.

"So why are we beating ourselves up?" Owen asked. "As far as I'm concerned, it's life as usual."

Asher couldn't agree with that. Because he believed Fiona this time. He was genuinely convinced Brock was history.

He recalled her face the last time they'd split. He and Owen had been kicked back at his place, watching a preseason game between the Ravens and the Saints when she'd shown up. Unlike after the previous breakups, she wasn't crying. Instead, she was pissed. She'd plopped down on the couch between them and sworn off Brock forever, promising the next guy she slept with was going to be the right one, the last one.

Then she'd calmed down, helped herself to a beer and kicked her feet up on the coffee table. She'd quietly murmured something about wishing she could find a guy like them, before settling in to watch the game.

Fiona got her love of sports from her family. She may not have grown up in Baltimore, but there seemed to be some sort of instilled devotion to the local teams passed down through the genes. She'd cussed the refs up one side and down the other every time they made a call against the Ravens.

While the game may have distracted Fiona, Asher couldn't stop thinking about turning toward her, gripping the back of her head and pulling her toward him for a kiss. It was the first moment he realized he wasn't in love with Christina.

Brock had been waiting at her place after the game, her entire apartment lit with hundreds of candles, a rose-petal path leading to the bedroom, and Eric F-ing Hutchinson—apparently a personal friend of Brock's—

playing the guitar and singing “Breakdown More” to her. Big Gesture Number 487.

“Shit,” Asher murmured, trying to knock the thought out of his head. The alcohol was impairing his better judgment. “Teddy’s right. We’re pathetic.”

Owen nodded. “So here’s the plan. There are only three women in the place worth braving that dance floor with. We’ll take turns dancing with Fiona and her cousins. It looks like Yvonne’s on a break and Sunnie just came back out of the kitchen.”

“Good call,” Asher said, standing up and weaving his way through several tables until he could reach out for Yvonne’s hand. Fiona’s cousin laughed as she tugged off her apron and jumped right into “Baby Got Back.” Yvonne appeared to know every single word, and he laughed as she rapped all the lyrics to him. The Collins women shared the same infectious sense of humor.

He looked over to see Owen had grabbed Fiona on her way back from the bathroom, and she was treating Owen to the same silly concert. Teddy and the bonbon were skirting the lines of public indecency with their bump and grind, and Asher chuckled when he caught a glimpse of Tris’s face, his eyebrows raised so high they nearly touched his hairline.

When the song changed, Owen handed Fiona off to him, pulling Sunnie away from the bar as Yvonne went back to work. Asher had gotten the better—or worse—end of the deal as a slow song came on.

Fiona stepped into his arms as if it were the most natural thing in the world. It probably was. Over the years, the two of them had shared countless dances at friends’ weddings, after-parties, birthday celebrations.

“I love this song,” she said as she placed her head against his chest. The lead singer was doing a pretty decent job with Ed Sheeran’s “Perfect”.

Fiona fit him perfectly. Her five-foot-six frame snuggled in just right against his six-one. Owen had him by an inch at six-two, and while it wasn't much, it meant he had a longer distance to travel to reach Fiona's plump, rosy lips.

Dammit. Again with the kissing.

"You really believe me?" Fiona asked.

"Yeah. I do."

She continued talking, her head still pressed against his chest. "His career will always come first, and as amazing as those big gestures were…they never lasted. It was this burst of closeness followed by months of distance—physically and emotionally. We never seemed to master the everyday routine of just enjoying each other's company. He was always too busy or away. And I know it sounds stupid, but I want that nothing-special day that's perfect because I'm with the person I love."

"You deserve to be someone's number one. Not just their close second."

Asher wasn't sure who moved first, but he looked down at the same time she tilted her head up. His nose brushed hers, they were so close, and she giggled. He didn't, so her quiet laugher died, her eyes going from amused to aroused in a single blink. Neither of them moved and for a moment, he got the strong sense that she *wanted* him to kiss her.

He could feel her hot breath on his face, the light scent of the beer they'd both been drinking, in the air between them. She licked her lips, drawing his attention to them.

Was that an invitation?

"Fee," he whispered.

The sound of her name on his lips seemed to break the spell, and they both moved back a few inches. Fiona gave him a sweet, guilty grin that made him wonder if she felt more than she was letting on. He glanced across the floor and saw Owen staring at them.

Owen was in love with her too. He and his best friend had it bad for the same girl. It was the unsolvable predicament.

Fiona, unruffled, put her head back against his chest and their slow swaying resumed. He tightened his hold as regret washed through him. Regret over the missed kiss. Suddenly it felt like things were about to take a turn, no matter how hard they tried to stick to the straight and narrow, to the tried and true. Asher wanted her so badly, it was a genuine physical pain.

The song was over too soon, and Owen came to steal her away. Asher needed a break so he returned to their booth, taking a long chug of Guinness. Maybe the beer would mute some of the shit rumbling around inside him.

He watched Owen and Fiona laugh as he spun her around. Damn woman loved to twirl around. It was impossible to be with her and not have fun. She was crazy, and she was making him the same.

"You going to let Owen slide in there without making an effort?" Teddy asked, slipping into the booth.

Asher looked around. "Where's the bonbon?"

Teddy crinkled his nose. "Pretty to look at, but dumb as owl shit. Was afraid I'd have to teach him how to unzip a zipper. Ain't nobody got time for that. Answer my question."

"There's too much to lose, Teddy. Him. Her. Us."

Teddy rolled his eyes so far back, Asher wondered if the gesture hurt. "Jesus, you wear me out. Show her Biggus Dickus and it's game over. You win."

Asher laughed, even as he shook his head. "My dick isn't that big, and that joke is as old as you trying to recruit me to your team."

"Biggus Dickus is *why* I'm trying to recruit you."

"I'm being serious here, man."

"So am I. I love Fiona more than my leather harness—and you know how I feel about that harness—and since I don't want to have sex with her and get married and make babies, I think she should be with you." Then he hesitantly added, "Or Owen."

"Which one of us?" Asher asked.

"I don't know. You'd both be great with her."

Asher nodded slowly. "Pretend you have to choose. Which one of us?"

Teddy frowned, glancing from Asher to Owen and back again. "I don't wanna choose."

Looking toward the dance floor, Asher watched Owen and Fiona attempting to "Wobble."

"So how do you expect us to ask Fiona to?" Asher asked.

"Fine. Be reasonable and responsible…as always. Or…throw caution to the wind. Did you ever consider Fiona might only be into *you*? After all, she and Owen already tried dating and he belly flopped…big time."

Asher took a swig of beer, studying the way Fiona looked at Owen, who was seriously fucking up the dance. It was similar to the expression she'd just flashed *his* way when he'd thought she wanted him to kiss her.

"Do you really think that's true?" Asher asked, even though he knew it wasn't. "That she doesn't still have feelings for him?"

"No. It's pretty obvious she loves both of you."

Asher's gaze flew to Teddy. "Did she say that?"

Teddy shook his head. "She didn't have to. I know that girl. She's been crazy about both of you for a long time. But she's just as stubborn and stupid as you are."

Asher sighed and leaned back in the booth, watching Owen and Fiona dance. For a second, he considered going out on the floor and joining them, basking in the fun that never ran dry when all of them were together.

"Hey," Teddy perked up. "I got it."

"Got what?"

"Your answer. Ménage."

Asher laughed. "How drunk are you?"

"Very. But that doesn't mean it's not a stellar idea."

Asher rolled his eyes. "Threesomes aren't really considered normal."

Teddy finished his beer. "No one in the world is normal. Not one single person. Hey, aren't those uncles we just met living in a committed threesome?"

Asher nodded. "Killian and Justin. Yeah. She's got another uncle, Sean, who's living with two partners too."

Teddy considered that for a second. "You know, the Collins family might be the closest to normal I've ever met. They're not paralyzed by their hang-ups, and they don't hide their flaws and kinks and crazy in the closet like the rest of us do. They own it. Embrace it."

Before Asher could reply to that, Owen and Fiona returned to the table. Teddy slid over to let Owen in and Fiona claimed the spot next to him.

"Where's the Bulgarian dude?" Owen asked Teddy.

"Had the IQ of a wet tea bag. Only capable of talking about himself, his hair and himself. In that order and on repeat."

Fiona grinned. "You told me once, everyone looks the same in the dark."

"It wasn't the looks that were the problem. It was the noise. Short of gouging my eardrums, I couldn't block out his stupid. It just kept spewing all over the table and polluting the air around us."

"Great imagery," Asher muttered.

"I'm a writer," Teddy replied with a wink.

"Did you finish my beer?" Fiona reached across the table for her empty mug.

"Oops." Teddy gestured toward the table he'd shared with his date. "Left mine over there."

"So it's back to Tinder?" she asked.

"Oh yeah. That was only strike one."

Tris stopped by the table with another pitcher and a clean mug for Teddy. Asher swore the guy was the greatest bartender on the planet. Nothing got by him. Then he tried not to groan as he considered drinking more beer.

"Someone wants to say hi," Tris said.

They had all been so preoccupied by the dancing, they hadn't seen Fiona's grandfather come in. Asher smiled when he saw the old guy walking toward them. Fee's Pop Pop was well over ninety, but no one would ever think of him as elderly. In fact, Asher imagined that in his day, he'd been every bit as intimidating as his son, Tris.

He sat up straighter as Fiona's grandfather smiled down at them, and Tris took over the introductions. "Pop, you remember Fiona's friends Asher and Owen, right?"

"Sure do," he said with a smile.

"And this is Teddy, the only one you've never met."

"Patrick Collins," he said, reaching out to shake his hand. "Fiona's told us so much about you, Teddy. Nice to finally meet you."

Asher expected Teddy to be his usual overly gregarious self, so he was surprised when his friend simply reached out and shook Patrick's hand, the picture of reverence and politeness.

"You too, Mr. Collins. Fee thinks the world of you."

Mr. Collins smiled and shook his head. "None of that Mr. Collins stuff. We're in the pub. In the pub, I'm Pat."

They chatted for a few minutes and then Patrick returned to his usual spot at the bar, surrounded by a group of men Fiona called his cronies. She filled their glasses once more from pitcher number…Asher didn't have a clue. Eight? Nine? Thirty-seven?

He was definitely skirting the line between wasted and drunk, which was the only explanation he had for almost kissing Fee on the dance floor. A sober Asher would have shown restraint.

They spent the next half hour discussing party plans, including what signature cocktail they could serve to match the theme. There were solid arguments made for both the Screaming Orgasm and Party Naked, until Asher pulled out his cell and found a recipe for an actual cocktail called Anything Goes that sounded pretty good. He'd tried to hang in there on the conversation, but too many times his thoughts had drifted back to Teddy's suggestion—the word threesome rolling round and round in his mind.

He dismissed it. For one thing, he was certain Fiona would never go for it. Well, he was pretty sure. Or…

Finally, he had to admit she probably wouldn't blink twice at the suggestion.

The problem was Owen…and him. Having a ménage sounded good in theory, but in practice? Asher wasn't sure he had it in him to share, but there was also very little he wouldn't do to protect his friendship with Owen…hell, with everyone at this table.

Fiona was the first to cry uncle. "We better go to bed and sleep this off or we're never gonna get any work done in the morning."

Owen winced. "By morning, you mean…one? Two o'clock in the afternoon, right?"

"I vote for waking up natural," Teddy said. "Everyone text when you wake up and when the last man standing gets out of bed, we'll reconvene here at the pub."

Asher shook his head. "No deal. We're working in the hotel suite. None of us is capable of self-control in a bar."

"Damn," Teddy muttered to Owen. "Thought I could slip that in unnoticed."

"We *are* on vacation," Fiona pointed out with a mischievous grin.

Owen laughed. "No worries. There's a minibar in the room."

Asher knew they were just jerking his chain, but he played his part, giving all of them the expected disapproving scowl.

As they rose, Owen and Teddy gave Fiona a hug and headed toward the door. He held back for a second.

"Thanks for the dance, Ash." She wrapped her arms around his waist and squeezed tightly. She was about to let go when the alcohol took over.

He reached around her shoulders, tugging her back against him and placing a kiss on the top of her head. She looked up at him with a confused expression and before he could think better of it, he leaned down and touched his lips to hers.

He wouldn't even call it a kiss because the second they touched, his brain engaged again and he pulled back.

Fiona didn't look shocked or appalled or even amused.

Instead, she tilted her head, and in that coy, adorable way she had, she said, "Little longer next time," before she turned away and walked toward the stairs to the Collins Dorm.

Owen and Teddy were both shaking their heads when he approached them, but he was in no mood for their teasing.

"Not. One. Word," he said through gritted teeth as he pushed between them and then the doorway to the sidewalk.

His friends followed. And for the first time in their lives, they actually did what he said.

Chapter Four

Fiona considered Asher's attempt at a kiss the whole way up the stairs.

What the hell was that?

What was messing with her even more was Owen on the dance floor. They'd danced together a thousand times, but tonight's dancing was something more, something hotter.

Once, when she turned around to mimic the bump and grind Teddy and his bonbon were doing next to them, she'd been shocked to realize Owen was sporting a serious erection. She started to move away, not wanting to make the situation awkward, but Owen grabbed her hips and suddenly the joke was on her as he pressed closer. Was he letting her know without words that what she'd felt was for her?

The whole night had been one what-the-fuck after another. And it had all started with her announcement that she'd dumped Brock.

Sunnie was hanging out with Colm and Lochlan when she got upstairs. Fiona lived alone in California, so she wasn't used to having people around all the time.

Sunnie took one look at her face and patted the spot on the couch next to her. "Uh-oh. What happened?"

"How do you know something happened?" she asked as she sat next to her cousin.

"Because when I left an hour ago, you were drunk as a skunk and laughing your ass off on the dance floor. Now you look like you've lost your best friend. Did you get into a fight with one of the guys?"

"Which guy?" Lochlan asked immediately.

Fiona hadn't needed to grow up here to still find herself enveloped in the protective arms of her male cousins, most notably Tris and Lane's twins, Padraig and Colm, and her oldest male cousin, Lochlan.

Lochlan was very much like his dad, Uncle Will. To outsiders, he appeared serious and stern and scary, but underneath the gruff exterior, there was a born warrior wrapped in pure marshmallow, the type of guy a girl definitely wanted at her back because he'd make her feel safe and adored and cared for all at the same time.

It was times like this when she understood Ailis's desire to live in Baltimore, to always be under this blanket of love and protection.

Although, when she considered it, she'd caught glimpses of that same warrior in Asher from time to time.

"I sort of wish we had gotten into a fight," she muttered. "That would be easier to understand."

Lochlan's scowl faded. "What do you mean?"

"I think my best friends have lost their minds."

Colm snickered. "I'm not trying to hurt your feelings, Fee, but are you sure Teddy has *ever* been sane? Dad was telling me some of the things he was saying to him and—"

She laughed. "He was the *only* person who was acting sane. Well…like his usual self tonight. Owen and Asher…"

"What about them?" Sunnie prompted.

"I told them I broke up with Brock on Valentine's Day—"

Sunnie interrupted. "You broke up with Brock? Six weeks ago? And we're only just hearing about it?"

Fiona was usually shit at keeping secrets, but she'd definitely held on to this one. Not only had she resisted telling her best friends, she hadn't spilled the beans to her family, either. Not even to her sister…and she told Ailis everything. "I wanted to be sure it would stick."

Sunnie grinned. "The big gesture?"

Fiona nodded.

"Well, I'm glad you dumped Tiny Cock Brock."

"You gave him a nickname?"

Sunnie shrugged. "Just now. All exes get nicknames."

Fiona laughed. "As much as I appreciate the comradery, I dumped him, so it's not like there was any broken-hearted crying scene. Besides, that name's not entirely accur—"

"Nah nah nah," Colm said loudly, fingers in his ears. "Don't bother to fix it. It's an insult that rhymes. That's all that matters."

Lochlan was frowning again. "So what happened with Owen and Asher?"

"They…" Fiona wasn't sure what to say. How much detail to go into. Usually the people she confided in were Teddy, Owen and Asher. But she could hardly do that, considering it was two-thirds of the group seriously messing with her head at the moment.

Then she had an epiphany. Wasn't this why she'd opted to stay in the Collins Dorm? To be a genuine part of the close-knit family for once? To take part in their game nights and movie marathons, and to be able to talk to them face-to-face about all the crap rolling around inside her head?

Colm leaned forward when she didn't immediately answer. "What's going on, Fee?"

"I think they were coming on to me."

"I knew it!" Sunnie lit up, holding out a hand to the guys. Fiona wasn't sure what to make of it when Lochlan and Colm both pulled out twenty-dollar bills and handed them to her.

"Pretty sure you cheated," Colm muttered.

"What are you doing?"

"I told them that Owen and Asher had the hots for you. Colm was pretty sure it was only Asher. Seems to think the guy's been pining for you forever. Lochlan's money was on Owen. Kept saying he never got over you after the breakup in college."

Fiona was flummoxed. Was it that obvious? And how had she missed the signs?

Because of Brock. She'd spent the past five years with her head stuck up her own ass, trying to figure out how to turn Mr. Big Gesture into Mr. Right. "You formed these opinions just tonight?"

Sunnie shook her head. "No. We made the bet tonight, when I came up and told the guys that things were getting hot and heavy downstairs. The basis for our opinions came from the times when you brought the guys home with you in the past. Although I sort of did have an advantage because I was in the pub earlier when you were dancing with both of them. Those were some pretty sexy dances."

"You didn't divulge that information," Colm said, eyeing the cash Sunnie quickly slid in the front pocket of her jeans. "You had an unfair advantage."

Sunnie shrugged unrepentantly. "You shouldn't have left after one drink."

"I was tired. I've been at work all day."

"You also shouldn't bet without knowing the odds." She tsked. "Pop Pop would be so disappointed if he knew."

Fiona laughed. "I can't believe you placed a bet on this."

Sunnie gave her a disbelieving look. "Seriously? We bet on everything."

Well…that was true.

"Gamblers Anonymous aside," Fiona said, "What the hell am I supposed to do about this?"

"Fuck them?" Sunnie asked. The answer was pure Aunt Riley.

"Helpful, Sun," Colm muttered, though his tone proved he didn't believe that at all.

"Why isn't that helpful? They're both hot *and* hot for her."

"I'm going to side with Colm on this. Sex fucks things up, and I'd like to keep them as my friends for…oh, I don't know—*forever*." Fiona leaned back against the couch and sighed.

Sunnie rolled her eyes. "Friends-schmends. Think how much *more* fun you could be having with them."

Fiona figured it spoke to the level of alcohol in her system that Sunnie sort of made sense. "That's true."

Sunnie smacked her thigh, happy to have proven her point. "Exactly. Take those two hotties to your bed, preferably together, and I *promise* you'll have fun."

"Together," Fiona murmured, her Guinness-soaked brain suddenly flaring with sexually graphic, gorgeous fantasies.

"Um, Fee." Lochlan leaned toward her. Her flushed cheeks must have given her away. "Ménages may not be weird in this family, but they are in most other places in the world. Are Owen and Asher the type who strike you as threesome guys?"

She laughed at the thought, his question dousing her fantasies like a bucket of ice water over flames. Jesus. If she'd thought having Owen—whom she'd slept with before—rubbing his erection against her on the dance floor was awkward, she didn't even want to consider what it would be like to have both guys naked with her at the same time.

She shook her head. "No. Not threesome guys. Hell, I'm not even sure I'm a threesome girl."

Colm, ever the lawyer, had already thought things through the next twenty-six steps. "Which means, if they *are* both interested, and you're interested as well, you'd have to choose."

Am I interested? In both of them?

She thought she might be.

"I can't do that. I can't choose."

Sunnie frowned. "So you're not even going to acknowledge their interest? I mean, they were both putting it out there tonight. Owen with that sexy bump and grind and Asher with that almost-kiss during the slow song."

"You really were paying attention," Fiona said.

At the same time, Colm muttered, "Cheater."

Fiona sighed. "There was actually a real, although super-quick kiss good night from Ash after you left." She blew out a long, frustrated breath. "I can't acknowledge this, Sunnie. Any of it. It could destroy the friendships."

Sunnie didn't seem to understand the concept of ignoring an obvious attraction, which wasn't surprising. She'd inherited more than her fair share of impulsiveness from her mother. She was an act-first-think-later kind of girl.

"That seems reasonable on the surface, but if the guys keep coming on to you, you may have to say something somewhere down the road. Nip it in the bud, so to speak," Colm said.

Fiona pouted. "I don't like it when you say stuff that's smart and rational."

He chuckled.

Then Lochlan took her by surprise. "Your reasons are sound, Fee. Protecting the friendships, guarding your heart and theirs. More than that, there's your work relationship to consider. You could break up the team."

Fiona bit her lower lip. "I know. And that scared me a lot. More than I can say."

Lochlan studied her face and grimaced. "Everything I said makes sense, but given the way you look right now, I think I might be on Sunnie's side on this."

Fiona hadn't expected that. "Seriously?"

"Nothing ventured, nothing gained. If you don't take a chance, what's the point? You want to be out there on the fifty-yard line, saying hike and grabbing the ball in your life? Or just standing on the sidelines, wishing you were in the game?"

"You're telling her to grab multiple balls," Colm said sardonically.

Lochlan started to deny that was his intention, but Sunnie talked louder and faster. "Oooo…double the balls," she said with a laugh. "You're only helping us make our point, Colm."

"I know." Lochlan shrugged. "I just can't stop thinking about Padraig. He could have protected his heart and walked away from Mia. Look at what he would have missed."

Colm crossed his arms, but didn't reply—either to agree or disagree.

Sunnie reached out and touched her knee. "Go for it, Fee. Otherwise, you might as well backslide to safe, boring Tiny Cock Brock."

Fiona shook her head. No matter what happened with Owen and Asher, she wasn't going back to Brock. So, she'd admit an attraction to both of them…and then what?

She circled back to the impossible problem. Owen and Asher wouldn't share. And she couldn't choose.

"You know," Sunnie said, her eyes lighting up. "I think I might have a way you could try this without much risk."

Colm snorted, the sound indicating he wasn't holding out much hope on the low-risk aspect.

Sunnie shot him a dirty look. "I'm being serious."

"I'm sure you are," Lochlan said, looking as dubious as Colm. "What's the plan?"

"Anything Goes."

Colm and Lochlan frowned, clearly confused, but Fiona got it. Immediately.

"Oh my God."

Her male cousins looked at her and Colm shook his head, still not catching on. "Oh my God, what?"

"The party on Saturday. Anything Goes," Fiona said, the answer completely appealing and exciting.

"Oh fuck. I forgot about that." Colm rested his elbows on his knees. "Listen, Fee. You need to think about this a little longer. And you need to approach the situation with a level—and sober—head."

Fiona had suggested the theme as a lark downstairs—before the dance and that split-second kiss—but now, it felt like the idea was fate smiling on her. "The party kills two birds with one stone. We were struggling with some aspects of the script, so trying it out might open up ideas we hadn't considered."

"Thought the show was written?" Colm said.

"The producer, Al, asked for some rewrites. Things that might be easier to fix with a little experience in the concept under our belts."

"I think I'm missing a step," Lochlan interjected. "I have no idea what this last show is about."

Fiona had spent the morning talking to Sunnie about the script for the season finale, and her cousin had fallen in love with the plot. Now Sunnie stood up, too excited to sit still. "The finale involves an anything goes night. The characters make all their decisions based on instinct, doing whatever they want to do without fear of consequences. We've already got the party planned. So all Fee has to do is follow her heart! Or at the very least, her hormones."

Colm rolled his eyes. "That's a terrible idea."

Fiona tried to decide who was right—Colm or Sunnie. The alcohol was definitely impairing her thought processes.

"We're doing the party," Sunnie said. "And everyone who comes commits to the theme."

"I'm not playing that game." Colm leaned back. "Fee, come on, you gotta be reasonable here. There's a big difference between sitcoms and real life. You can call the night anything you want, but there will be consequences come morning. Actually, all those reasons you listed for not pursuing Owen and Asher will still be there. This isn't going to fix anything."

Fiona had just enough alcohol left in her system to feel contrary. Between the booze and the horniness, common sense wasn't as appealing as Sunnie's suggestion. "I like the idea. I'll flirt, check out their moves and see where the night leads. It might actually make it obvious to all of us which guy is the right one, and then there would be no hard feelings. This could work."

Lucky for her, Teddy was gay or she'd *really* be in a pickle.

"It's not going to work," Colm muttered.

"Why don't you sleep on it, Fiona?" Lochlan suggested.

Fiona grinned. "No good ever comes from sleeping on an idea."

Colm rubbed his forehead. "Said no one ever."

"I'm kidding, Lochlan. There are two days between now and the party, and I'm pretty damn sure I'll change my mind four hundred times in between."

Colm crossed his arms. "Good. Change it the right way and all will be well."

Fiona looked at Sunnie. "Are they always this stodgy?"

Sunnie blew out an exasperated breath. "You have no idea. They're impossible to reason with."

Lochlan laughed. "What a female Collins considers reason is the polar opposite to the way the males in this family think."

"Which is why we always have so much fun together," Sunnie added, as if that should be obvious to everyone.

Lochlan shrugged good-naturedly. "Going to have to give you that one, Sun."

Colm rose from his chair. "And that's my cue to leave. When Sunnie starts making sense, it's time to run. I'm going back downstairs for another drink. Lochlan, you want to join me?"

Lochlan stood as well. "I think that's a good idea."

"Can I get a promise from you, Fiona?" Colm asked.

She crinkled her nose. "Do I have to?"

"It's just a small one. Sleep on this idea. Get the alcohol out of your system first and then decide with a clear head. Okay? Please."

She sighed. "Okay. But you have to promise me something in return. Both of you."

"What?" Colm asked.

“You have to agree to come to the party and play the game. One night. Anything Goes.” She recalled Sunnie’s enthusiasm earlier, so she stole her descriptor. “It’s going to be epic.”

“Yeah,” Colm said. “That’s what I’m afraid of.”

“So you’ll come?” Fiona pressed.

Lochlan nodded. “We’ll be there.”

“Anything Goes,” Colm said quietly as he and Lochlan left the room. “Jesus. This isn’t going to end well for anyone.”

Chapter Five

"Are you guys finished fucking around now?" Teddy asked the second they left the hotel suite the next afternoon. It had been a very sleepy start, with Fiona the last to wake naturally. She had just texted and suggested a late lunch at Sunday's Side before they started working. Her exact words were, "I need something in my stomach to soak up the leftover alcohol. Riley made biscuits and gravy."

Asher looked at Owen and wondered which of them looked more frustrated. It was obvious his friend hadn't slept any better than he had. Something had shaken loose last night—thanks to Fiona's bombshell about the breakup and the Guinness-soaked conversations afterwards—and Asher didn't have a clue what to do about it. Which was unnerving because, as his friends were fond of pointing out, he was always a man with a plan.

"It's not that simple, Ted," Asher said after a tense minute.

Teddy snorted. "Tell me about it. You're both gunning for the same girl. And it's Fee. This shit can't happen, man. If you fuck up our perfect lives, I'll kill you. All three of you."

They *were* living pretty perfect lives—professionally—and they all knew it. They were at the top of their game. Owen had gotten close to a dozen scripts in the past year with offers to star in movies, while he, Teddy and Fiona had all received some pretty sweet offers for other writing gigs in Hollywood. Add in the fact they got to work together all day, every day, laughing their asses off as they did something they truly loved, and it was hard to argue with Teddy.

The problem was…their personal lives weren't quite as perfect. Not that any of them were dreadfully unhappy on that front. But there was no denying all of them had that sense of something missing. Owen and Teddy filled that hole with hookups, while he and Fiona plugged it with work.

"We're not going to fuck it up," Asher said, praying those words weren't a lie. He sensed Owen's gaze on him as they walked, so he bit the bullet and forced himself to face his friend. "We won't."

Owen gave him a disbelieving smile and they continued walking. Asher could understand his reticence, his fears. Owen had spent most of childhood being shuffled from one disinterested relative to the next after his mom died of an overdose. His deadbeat dad had been in prison since Owen was four, so he'd never known him. Owen had confided once that it wasn't until he'd landed a scholarship to USC, opting to be the triple in a dorm to save money, that he really understood what it was like to have good friends and people who cared about him.

Asher had met Fiona, Owen and Teddy in English 101, and the four of them had been inseparable from day one of freshman year. Literally day one.

Owen had fallen for Fiona just as fast as he had. The difference was, Owen had asked her out, and the two of them had embarked on what she wasn't wrong to call their three-minute relationship. They'd started dating at the end of September their sophomore year and had broken it off by early December. They'd both been nineteen, impulsive and prone to drama.

"Never thought I'd say this, but I'm sort of praying for Brock to come through with one of his big gestures." Teddy ran his hand through his shaggy, curly blond hair. The dude was working on a white-boy afro and it was in serious need of a cut, but Teddy was terrible at making and keeping appointments. Asher would have to ask Tris if there was a barbershop nearby.

"Don't think it would matter if he did," Owen said. "I believe her. It's over this time."

Asher believed her too. He wasn't sure what the difference was, but there was something in her face when she'd talked about Brock last night. Whatever she felt for the man in the past was gone.

Then he realized what the difference was. She'd looked and sounded like *he* did after he'd split up with Christina. Much as it pained him to admit—even to himself—he had heard it in her tone.

"I shouldn't have kissed her," Asher confessed. That had weighed heavy on him all night. He'd done it right in front of Owen.

"Wait," Teddy said with a laugh. "You're calling that fuckup from last night a kiss? I've gotten more action from my aunt Gladys on Christmas Day."

Owen snorted out a laugh. "Your problem was the setting. You were in the pub surrounded by a million of her overprotective uncles."

Funny. Asher had never considered that. He'd been too worried about Owen's reaction to contemplate her family's response.

"Why didn't you just lure her under the mistletoe over the holidays like I did?" Owen asked.

Asher stopped walking. “Maybe because she was still dating Brock and I was with Christina.”

Owen shook his head. “Wasted opportunity if you ask me, considering how those two relationships turned out. She looked hot in that red cashmere sweater.”

Owen lived his life in the gray area. Hell, Asher wasn’t sure Owen had realized there were hard and fast rules about right and wrong until they’d met in college. As such, Owen referred to him as the eternal Boy Scout.

Owen’s family was about as different from the Collins family—and Asher’s single, overprotective, “my son walks on water” mom—as it got. Fiona and Asher had grown up surrounded by supportive, loving adults, but there had been precious few of that type in Owen’s childhood.

So, Owen had lured his in-a-relationship friend under the mistletoe and kissed her—with tongue. She’d given him shit for it afterwards, but Asher noticed she hadn’t held back during the kiss. And she definitely hadn’t pushed Owen away.

Fiona was like Owen. Fond of the gray area.

Asher almost wished he was a big enough man to stand down, to tell Owen to go for it. Because there was no denying Owen would be good to her. He’d give her everything she deserved, and she’d be the perfect wife for him. Owen would thrive under her love.

Shouldn’t he want that for Owen? For Fiona?

Maybe.

But he knew his own heart too. Knew there was no way he could step aside. Fiona had turned his head when he’d been eighteen years old and no one, not even Christina, had changed that.

“Been thinking about tomorrow’s party,” Owen said.

Teddy stopped walking, so they all halted. It was probably better they had this conversation before they hit the restaurant where Fiona was waiting for them.

"Thinking about it how?" Teddy asked.

"Anything Goes sort of leaves the door open to a hell of a lot."

Asher blew out a long breath. "Stop talking." There was no malice behind his words. But the fact was he'd been thinking about that party too. A lot.

"What?" Owen asked.

"You can't discuss or plan Anything Goes. You just walk in the room and let all inhibitions go. You become exactly who you've always wanted to be with nothing holding you back. Not fear, not past history, not…friendships."

Owen listened, and Asher knew he was already miles ahead of his friend on this.

"Yeah," Owen said slowly. "You're right."

Asher caught his eye. "What we should probably discuss is the morning after."

"No," Owen disagreed. "What happens Saturday night happens. On Sunday morning, we go right back to where we are now…if we want to. If we don't…"

Teddy closed his eyes and groaned. "Fuck me. I'm not looking forward to Sunday. I can't deal with all this angst on a hangover a second time. It's pretty much killing me to listen to it now." Then he opened his eyes and shook his head in a way that told them Teddy thought they were both morons. "Come on. There's absolutely nothing I can do to stop this, so let's just get on with it." He walked toward the restaurant, a few steps ahead of them, muttering, "Knew things were too good to be true."

Asher looked at Owen. "You're always going to be my best friend."

He smiled. "You're my brother, man. We just have to believe things are going to work out the way they were meant to be."

"You're right."

Owen headed to the restaurant again and Asher followed.

Teddy had already claimed the spot next to Fiona in the booth when he and Owen arrived. He rolled his eyes at their friend's attempt to keep them separated from Fiona.

For someone who said she was hungover, Fiona had never looked prettier. Her dark auburn hair was pinned back in a high ponytail, and she had taken the time to swipe on some mascara and lipstick, though not much else. Not that she needed it. She had porcelain skin that never lost its light tan, thanks to her time in the sun. Her exercise of choice was running, and she typically started her day by jogging around a neighborhood park. The morning sun softly bronzed her skin and pulled out the smattering of adorable freckles on her cheeks and nose that she hated.

They sat down and Fiona's uncle Ewan walked over to the table to say hello and take their orders.

"Bit shorthanded this afternoon. Two of my waitresses have come down with bad head colds. I told them to stay home. Yvonne tells me the four of you had a good time last night at the pub."

"Too much fun," Fiona said, rubbing her head. "Today, we're all business. We've got a ton of work to do."

Ewan humphed. "That's a shame. Karaoke night at the pub. Always a great time. Sean started it years ago, but Tris called a halt to it after a while, claiming it was the cruelest form of torture. Padraig brought it back over the summer for Mia, and we've been doing it the last Friday of every month ever since. Patrons love it and it's always good for a laugh. Tris just makes sure he's off that night. Although..." Ewan chuckled. "With Paddy out of town, he's covering tonight. Which is actually a bonus for the rest of us. His expressions when some of the singers take the stage are worth the price of admission."

Asher recalled meeting all of Fiona's uncles during a summer break when they were twenty and had traveled to Baltimore for a long weekend. Her family was holding an end-of-summer bash at a nearby park on the waterfront. He'd been intimidated by the guys, until he'd seen the way they were big old teddy bears around their wives, sisters and nieces. Asher had never really understood the meaning of overprotective dads—growing up with only his mom—until he'd spent those few days with the Collins men. He had watched and learned, taking it to heart when Fiona's cousin Colm had pulled him aside and told him to keep an eye on her at college for them.

He'd given Colm his promise and hadn't broken it since.

Teddy's eyes lit up. "Karaoke?"

Owen shook his head. "Forget it."

"Actually," Asher said, an idea forming, "I don't think we should forget it."

Owen looked at him in shock. "Seriously? You're the last person I would ever expect to go for karaoke."

"I don't want to sing, but think about it, Owen. Karaoke would be hilarious in the script. Al's struggling with your character's progression that night. What if we threw Wild Winters on stage with a mic?"

"Oh my God! Yes!" Fiona raised her hand, and she and Asher fist bumped. "It's perfect," she exclaimed.

Ewan laughed. "Does this mean I should save you a table on the bar side tonight?"

Teddy nodded, answering for all of them before Owen could continue his argument. “Absolutely.”

They ordered their late lunch and ate, then decided to venture upstairs to the apartment rather than heading back to the hotel. None of them seemed motivated to open a laptop, and Asher could only assume it was because he and Owen were distracted by Fiona and the upcoming party, and Teddy was knee-deep in texts, after finding his second Tinder true love—some guy named Brian or Ryan or… Asher had only half listened because Teddy could go on forever about pretty much every subject in the world and, after a while, his voice turned to white noise in the background.

Sunnie and Finn were upstairs when they arrived, so the six of them hung out and watched *Chopped*, talking about little bits of everything, including the party, what songs they should sing at karaoke, what other members of the Collins family were up to, and Hollywood gossip. It was the perfect afternoon.

As soon as the sun set, Teddy insisted they go to the pub to grab their table. When they got downstairs, Asher was glad Ewan had saved them a spot, as the place was already packed. They were sitting at a big table with Fiona’s uncles Sean and Chad, and their wife, Lauren. Sunnie and Finn had both been recruited to work, since Padraig was still gone. Tris really had broken his vow to remain away and was filling a pitcher from the tap behind the long counter as they sat down, his face the very definition of grumpy.

Asher claimed the chair on Fiona’s left, Owen taking the right before Teddy could attempt to run interference. Not that he’d tried. He’d taken one look at Sean and grabbed the free chair next to him, doing precious little to hide his instant crush despite the fact the man’s partners were right there at the table.

"You guys are in for a real treat," Sean said enthusiastically.

Chad snorted. "Not sure 'treat' is the word I'd use."

Lauren sat between the men, sipping on a glass of wine. "For the record, I'm not getting up there tonight. Last time we were here, you both let me drink too much of this," she lifted her glass, "then allowed me to make a complete ass of myself onstage."

Sean looked wounded by her accusation. "You're kidding, right? You sang '9 to 5' better than Dolly could ever hope to."

Lauren winced. "God. Don't remind me."

They all laughed when Chad plucked a bottle of white wine from the ice bucket on their table and topped up Lauren's glass.

"Asshole," she muttered, though she was smiling at her husband.

Asher was fascinated by the dynamics of their relationship. He'd watched the three of them quite a bit on his first trip to Baltimore with Fiona, curious about their unconventional marriage and how they made it work. And there was no denying it worked well. They'd been married for well over twenty years, and the way they sat close to each other, touching, laughing, and joking, proved it was definitely a happy union.

Yvonne came by to take their drink orders, the men opting for a couple pitchers of National Bohemian, and Fiona took Lauren up on her offer to share the wine.

"Are you fellas planning to sing?" Sean asked, reaching around to borrow a song list from a nearby table.

Asher grabbed the list. "Owen is."

Owen narrowed his eyes. "Correction. We all are."

Fiona leaned close to Asher, reading the song titles. "Woot! Got mine." She was up and out of the chair within seconds to place her song request with the guy running the karaoke machine.

"Shit," Owen cursed. "Give me the list." He scanned it several times, then stood to put his name in as well.

Asher studied the song choices, but his gaze kept coming back to one song. He looked at Owen, standing with Fiona in line, and decided *fuck it.* He rose and hopped in the line of people waiting at the table to sign up.

Owen was clearly surprised when he turned and discovered Asher directly behind him in line. "Seriously? I figured you'd find a way to back out."

Asher shrugged. "Found a song on the list I like. And you're right. If I'm making you do it, it's only fair I take a turn too."

Owen nodded slowly. "Yeah. Okay."

Teddy appeared behind them, grinning from ear to ear. "Got my song picked out too."

Once they'd all signed up, they returned to the table, the conversation flowing easily as Chad and Lauren asked questions about the show and the cast and the finale they planned to film at the bar.

Teddy had managed to draw Sean into a conversation about Mexican food, the two of them debating which was better—soft or hard tacos. While Teddy's sexual innuendoes about liking things hard were obvious to everyone at the table, Sean played the straight man, pretending they really were just talking about food. Asher hoped Owen and Fiona were taking mental notes, because they had to turn this into a sketch for next season's show.

Fiona's name was called first, and Asher was surprised when Yvonne and Sunnie hopped onstage, taking their places as her backup singers. Then she launched into a legit rendition of Fergie's 'Clumsy.'

"Wow," Asher said, his eyes glued to Fiona.

She owned the stage—holding the entire pub captive with her sexy voice and provocative dance moves. Actually, Asher figured it was all three women—the perfect match set with Fee's red hair, Yvonne's brunette and Sunnie's blonde tresses—catching everyone's attention.

Sean looked over at him with a proud uncle grin. "Our family makes amazing girls. As Colonel Potter from *MASH* used to say about his family, there's not a bum in the lot."

Asher agreed. Then he glanced around the room and recognized the same affection on the faces of Tris, Finn and Pop Pop.

Owen had bumped over into the chair next to him. He must have seen the same Collins pride radiating. "No one in my family ever looked at *me* like that, like the sun rose and set on my shoulders. I can't even begin to imagine what it would feel like to have someone love me—"

Owen stopped short, and Asher wasn't sure how to respond to his friend's revealing comment. It was rare when Owen talked about his family, the slipups typically only happening when he was three sheets to the wind. Which he wasn't at the moment. Asher had noticed the guy was quieter today, his usual swagger and flamboyance dimmed.

Teddy was looking in their direction and from the frown on his face, it was apparent he'd overheard Owen. Like him, Teddy didn't appear to know what to say, either.

Asher looked back at Fiona and realized she was looking at him. She gave him an adorable wink as she sang the chorus.

Shaking off his brief melancholy, Owen put two fingers in his mouth and blew out the "hot stuff" whistle that delighted her. Asher put his finger in his ear, feigning a wince, pretending Owen had deafened him.

Lauren, Sean and Chad were into the song as well, mouthing the words, chair dancing with each other, laughing. The three of them reminded him of the relationship he shared with Owen, Fiona and Teddy. Friendship merged with love. The only difference was, Sean and his partners shared an incredible physical attraction as well. It was captivating to watch as well as unnerving. Asher couldn't quite put his finger on it, but watching the three of them caused his chest to tighten.

He glanced over and realized Owen was watching the trio too, smiling at them because Teddy was on a roll and had Sean, Chad and Lauren in stitches.

Then Owen turned toward him—and Asher's chest constricted even more. He found it hard to breathe, but he couldn't figure out why. It felt a bit like a panic attack.

They were embarking on something new, something really risky and completely out of character for all of them, so that could explain the sudden wave of angst.

Owen noticed his distress, because his smile faded and his forehead creased. He might have said something if Fiona's song hadn't ended and Owen's name was called to come to the stage.

Owen appeared to regret his song choice the second the music started. After all, there was a definite "Jessie's Girl" vibe in their group at the moment. Leave it to Owen to impulsively choose the song as a joke without thinking it through. His discomfiture was apparent when he sang the first verse without looking toward their table. Instead, it looked like he was trying to channel his television character. The character Wild Winters was the product of hippies, a free spirit who always brought chaos to his circle of straight-laced friends.

Owen joked that Teddy was actually the inspiration for his character, which was no surprise to any of them. So Owen put on a show, singing with too much emotion, painting his face with over-the-top pained expressions the way Teddy would, all for a laugh.

But when Owen reached the chorus, he didn't avoid them any longer. His eyes landed on Fiona first, who was laughing at his antics, singing along and cheering loudly. Asher wondered if his friend had purposely sought her out because her response was the only easy one. She didn't know about the tug-of-war he and Asher were currently engaged in as they both hoped to win her heart.

Owen looked at Asher next, and he tried to ease his friend's agitation by rolling his eyes and smiling. Then Owen found Teddy, who was kicked back in his chair, his arms crossed, a thoughtful expression on his face.

Owen looked away when the second verse kicked in, and he had to glance back at the computer monitor for the words. He finished the song and was treated to a standing ovation at the end, something Asher was sure he'd earned because of who he was, not how well he sang.

He reclaimed his seat at the table, careful to avoid Asher's eyes. Sean praised him for his performance, but the accolades died quickly when Teddy's name was called.

"Oh my God," Fiona muttered when Teddy launched into the most hilarious rendition of "It's Raining Men" in history.

"Jesus. I'm glad I didn't have to sing after him," Owen said between laughs.

Sean, Chad and Lauren were doubled over, tears streaming from their eyes.

"That guy," Sean said, unable to catch his breath.

"I can see why you're friends with him," Chad interjected when Sean simply continued to guffaw.

When his song ended, Teddy didn't make it back to his seat, as several patrons called him over to the bar, buying him shots for his solid-gold concert.

A couple other singers took their turns on the stage, but the songs paled in comparison to Teddy's act. Sean, Lauren and Chad excused themselves to head over to Sunday's Side to chat with Keira and Riley, who were watching the show from the double doors between the restaurant and the pub.

"Is that the song you want Wild Winters to sing on the show?" Fiona asked.

Owen shook his head. "No. I just picked the first title I saw on the list that I knew. We can give more thought to what Wild sings, find something that ties in better with the plot."

"Cool." Fiona lifted the song sheet from the table. "Maybe something on here will spark some ideas."

Asher leaned toward Fiona, resting his arm along the back of her chair as he peered at the list with her. Owen watched as Asher twisted a few strands of her hair around his finger, playing with it in a way that was more flirt than friend.

They'd both agreed to let the cards fall where they may, but that idea was far from fleshed out. In fact, it was borderline stupid.

Okay. It *was* stupid.

None of that mattered when Fiona leaned toward him, curling into his hold. Asher dropped her hair, his fingers slowly gliding along her neck. She shivered lightly at the touch but didn't look up from the paper. It didn't take a genius to realize neither one of them was reading the damn thing. Her face flushed a soft pink as he continued to stroke the side of his neck.

Owen didn't try to get in the game, but he didn't move, didn't look away. Asher glanced in his direction, wishing he could figure out what his friend was thinking.

Asher suspected the three of them could have remained there, locked together, anticipating what would happen next, but the spell was broken by the deejay when he called out his name.

He didn't move for the count of at least five, unhappy about walking away. Fiona was the first to shake free.

"Your turn, McCarthy," she said, her voice suddenly huskier than it had been a few minutes before.

Asher's dick responded. Dammit. He tried to subtly adjust his jeans as he walked to the stage.

***

If anyone had told Owen that Asher McCarthy would steal the show on karaoke night a few hours ago, Owen would have laughed them out of the pub.

Now…

Owen knew Asher had a decent singing voice. After all, he'd heard the other man jamming in the shower back when they'd shared a dorm room. But Asher had never let loose, never revealed this soulful side. He'd selected one of Owen's favorite songs, "Budapest," singing it as good as—if not better than—George Ezra.

And unlike him, Asher didn't pretend there wasn't a deeper meaning hidden in his song choice. His eyes were locked on Fiona. Her light blush deepened, but she didn't attempt to hide it. Her sweet smile grew as Asher continued to serenade her, and Owen watched her reaction, awestruck by how truly touching this moment was.

Seeing Asher stroke Fiona's neck, watching their obvious attraction, had awakened something in Owen. Something he was struggling to contain.

Toward the end of the song, Owen forced himself to look back at the stage. He was surprised when Asher's attention turned to him as he sang, "give me one good reason why I should never make a change," before he focused on Fiona once more.

"I've got a boner the size of Florida," Teddy said as he reclaimed his seat, and Owen forced a laugh. He was suffering from the same affliction after watching Asher with Fiona. Asher's song had ended and several of the tipsier women had made their way to the stage, flirting and offering to buy him drinks. Predictable as always, Asher politely declined all offers.

"Where the hell did *that* guy come from?" Teddy asked Asher as he returned to the table.

"What guy?"

"Sex incarnate! Jesus, man. Come to the dark side. I'm begging you."

Asher laughed. "Sorry, Ted. Princess Leia just dumped her Stormtrooper." He looked at Fiona, who was clearly aghast by Asher's outright declaration. "Gotta take my shot before the next big gesture comes along."

Fiona tilted her head. "How much have you had to drink tonight?"

"Two beers. I'm not drunk. By the way, Owen's tossing his hat in the ring too."

Now it was Owen's turn to sit there with his mouth hanging open. "What the hell are you saying, man?"

Teddy, who was never without a million words, sat there absolutely speechless, which meant the bomb Asher dropped was followed by a painfully long silence.

Fiona stood when it continued. "I…I…"

"No, Fee," Asher said, cutting her off. "Don't say anything tonight. Or tomorrow night. We'll revisit this conversation Sunday morning. After the Anything Goes party."

"The party," she whispered.

Owen shook himself from his stupor. Asher had opened a door and Owen didn't have a clue how to close it. Or even know if he even should.

Owen stood as well, then leaned toward her, searching for the right response. She lifted her face to his, so he gave her the kiss she seemed to be inviting. He'd intended to keep it quick, but she tasted good, her breath flavored by Chardonnay and sweet chocolate from the dessert they'd all split earlier.

She was the first to break away, and it was then he realized Asher was standing now too. Fiona turned toward him with a guilty grin. "Why do I feel like we're driving a hundred miles an hour toward a brick wall?"

"Because you are," Teddy muttered, his expression black.

Teddy was angry, and that rage only grew when Fiona looked at Asher and said, "Is it worse that I don't care?"

Teddy huffed out a soft sound of disgust, then picked up his beer to take a big swig, mumbling something about being surrounded by a pack of fools.

Asher ran his knuckles along Fiona's cheek. "We'll see you tomorrow night at the party."

She nodded, and Owen could tell she was waiting to see if Asher would give her a good-night kiss as well. When he didn't move to initiate one, she gave them an adorable finger wave and headed toward the stairs that would take her to the apartment above.

"Have you lost your mind?" Owen asked Asher, who shook his head.

"Nope. I just figured a few things out. I got a good feeling about this."

Owen snorted. "Well, I'm glad *you* do. Because I'm with Fee on this. We're barreling straight toward our doom." He dropped back down in his chair.

The smile never faded from Asher's face as he said, "trust me," before turning toward the bar to pay their tab.

"What the fuck is going on?" Owen asked Teddy when they were alone.

Teddy nodded slowly. "I think Asher just opened the door for you, him and her to have a threesome."

"I'm not a threesome guy."

He hadn't meant the words as a joke, but Teddy reacted as if he'd just said the funniest thing ever. "Well, I suggest you do some research before tomorrow night."

"I'm being serious, man." Owen's stomach clenched at the thought of what Asher was proposing.

Teddy reached over and placed a comforting hand on his shoulder. "I know you are, Owen, but I can't help you make this decision. It has to be yours. You know that, right?"

Owen nodded—and accepted that he wasn't going to get a minute's sleep tonight.

For better or worse, everything changed tomorrow.

Chapter Six

Teddy cornered Asher three seconds after Owen got in the shower to get ready for the party.

"What are you up to?"

Asher didn't bother to pretend he didn't understand the question. "I started thinking about that Anything Goes concept when Fiona originally suggested the idea. Indulged in a few fantasies about what mine would involve. Truth is, I never thought I'd get the chance to act on them."

"And Owen was in the bedroom with you and Fee during these fantasies?"

Asher shook his head. "No. But I've been thinking about it since Thursday night."

"There's a difference between thinking and fantasizing."

"Yeah," Asher admitted, "I know that."

Teddy perched himself on the edge of the coffee table in the living room of their suite. He'd invited Ryan to the party and had been a bundle of nervous energy ever since the other man accepted. "If you have sex with Owen, I'll cut my dick off and live life as a eunuch."

Typical dramatic Teddy response.

"How long are you going to pretend to have a crush on me?" Asher asked.

"I stopped pretending it was a crush in college. These days I've upped my game—now I pretend I'm madly in love with you. More of a challenge for me and it gets bigger laughs."

Asher sat on the couch and propped his feet up on the coffee table next to Teddy. "I'm not sleeping with Owen."

"But you don't mind if Fee does…as long as you're in the bed too?"

"I was watching Sean, Chad and Lauren last night, and—"

"Who are Chad and Lauren?" Teddy joked.

"You gotta stop coming on to Fiona's uncles, man. I'm not sure she finds it funny."

Teddy waved his concern away. "She loves it. Besides, unlike straight Tris, Sean's bi. Thought I might actually have a shot there."

Asher lifted one brow.

Teddy chuckled, conceding. "If he weren't in love with Chad. And Lauren. Who were both at the table with us. So you were watching them last night and…" Teddy was the king of affected pauses.

"I saw an answer to an unsolvable problem."

Teddy rubbed his jaw. "Doesn't mean it's the right answer."

"You suggested it."

"I was drunk as a skunk. And joking."

"I know."

"You realize you blindsided Owen last night. He was still thinking tonight would be a free-for-all, winner-takes-all deal. Then you went and threw him into a ménage scenario."

"Yeah. Part of me thinks I'm pushing too hard, moving too fast. Then I think about watching her with

Brock the last five years, and I remember it's been a lifetime of waiting."

Teddy tilted his head. "You weren't waiting alone for a few of those. Christina—"

"I was never in love with her. You know that."

"I do. What happens if Owen bucks the threesome idea?"

Asher ran a hand through his hair. "I don't know." Given Owen's upbringing and the feelings he shared last night about wanting someone to love him, Asher was more determined than ever to make tonight work. Asher was in love with Fiona, and if the only way he could have her without breaking his best friend's heart was to share her, then so be it.

"Don't you think you should figure that out?" Teddy asked.

"You know what? No. I'm tired of planning everything down to the nth degree and then telling everyone what to do. Everybody gets to be impulsive but me. Fiona buys shoes the way some people buy food. Owen jets off for ski weekends whenever there's fresh powder just because he wants to. You pick out guys on Tinder based on no more than their looks. Why can't I do something crazy…just for the hell of it?"

"Because you're not crazy. And this is. Besides, I'm not sure Owen is as impulsive as you're giving him credit for. Skiing is a lot different than orgies."

"It's not an orgy, and I don't care. I'm not giving him time to reject the idea before we've tried it."

Teddy laughed. "Jesus. I never realized what an effect I was having on you until this moment. I've clearly been a bad influence. Tell you what. Take a few minutes in the shower to play out the fantasy…with a naked Owen as part of the scenario. You can't just dream about you and Fee. If you're determined to see this through, you'd better be ready to walk the walk.

But no boy touching between you two. I mean it. I've been in line for that way longer than both you fuckers."

"That's not going to be a problem."

Teddy didn't seem convinced…which threw Asher off-balance. He had always thought Teddy was joking about the crush on him, but for a second, Asher got the sense his friend was genuinely jealous.

"I'm serious, Ted."

Teddy nodded. "I know you are."

"Is there something else bothering you?"

"I'm just not sure mixing Owen's TV-star ego with your control-freak nature will make for an easy blend in the bedroom."

Asher leaned forward, resting his elbows on his thighs. "You think we'll be fighting to be in charge?"

"Fuck no. Fiona's got that gig wrapped up."

Asher laughed, but didn't disagree. "You think I'm making a mistake." He didn't bother to turn his comment into a question. He could tell Teddy had more than a few doubts.

His friend's response surprised him. "If anyone could find a way to take a perfect friendship and make it more, it would be you, Asher. And if you succeed…everyone is happy."

For some strange reason, Asher got a sense that Teddy wasn't including himself in that "everyone."

If you succeed…

Teddy's words were still ringing in his ears as they climbed the stairs to the Collins Dorm later that night. They could hear the music as they reached the top, mingled with lots of loud voices, and the smell of…

"Bacon!" Teddy cried out as they entered. He made a mad dash for the dining room and Asher and Owen started to follow, but they stopped when Fiona approached them.

"You're here."

Asher nodded slowly as he let his gaze travel along the length of her. She'd pinned two lengths of hair back, leaving the majority of it loose. There was a tiara nestled amongst the auburn tresses. That was all normal enough for her. She kept three tiaras in her desk drawer at work just for shits and giggles and wore them more often than Asher figured was probably natural.

It was the rest of her outfit that blindsided him.

"Belle?" Owen asked.

Fiona giggled as she lifted the skirt on her bright yellow dress and twirled. Her shoulders were bare from the off-the-shoulder style of the ball gown, and her little pirouette revealed the matching yellow slippers underneath.

"Did we say it was a costume party?" Asher asked.

Fiona gave him an incredulous look. "Um…it's an Anything Goes party," she explained as if he'd missed the memo. "I'm pretty sure costumes were implied."

"I feel like I want a do-over," Owen said. "I'd rock a *Magic Mike* look."

"Oooo," Fiona said, her eyes widening in approval. "Go home and change. We can wait. Or better yet…let me find the appropriate music and you can get into character here." She reached out, tugging his T-shirt from his jeans.

Owen laughed—until her hands slid beneath the cotton to his waist. "Um, Fee…"

"Hitting the ground running, are we?" Asher asked, stepping behind Fiona to sandwich her between him and Owen. "I like it," he whispered in her ear.

He and Owen exchanged glances for the briefest of seconds and once again, Asher struggled to read Owen's expression, which was somewhere between aroused and deer in the headlights.

The moment ended when Teddy called out, "You guys have got to come see this!"

Owen took a step back until Fiona's hands fell away, then he headed toward their friend.

Asher wasn't so quick to give up his spot. Neither was Fiona.

She leaned back against him.

"I like your dress."

She laughed, then turned to face him. "You really think this will work?"

"I have no idea what you mean." He played dumb, waiting to see if she'd give him some indication of her own feelings.

Unfortunately, Fiona never showed her hand too quickly. It was why he'd stopped playing poker with her. She studied his face, waiting instead for him to reveal something.

He was tempted, but it was too early in the night. Asher reached up to cup her face with both hands. "You look beautiful."

Fiona leaned toward him, but he resisted the urge to kiss her. There was plenty of time for that when it was just the three of them. He released her with a quick peck on the tip of her nose that irritated her, given her sudden scowl, then he went to join Owen and Teddy.

The second he saw the dining room table, he understood Teddy's excitement. Sunnie had outdone herself with the food.

"Holy heart attack," he murmured.

"It's perfect and you know it," Sunnie said, walking up behind him. Like her cousin, she'd opted for Disney princess.

"Greetings, Jasmine," Asher said. "Nice veil."

"I can't believe we didn't think of costumes," Teddy grumbled.

"*Magic Mike*, right?" Owen asked.

Teddy's eyes widened at the suggestion. "We're going to have this party over again next weekend. We fucked up royally. I'll be Channing Tatum and you can be Matthew McConaughey."

Owen scowled. "I'm Joe Manganiello and you know it." He tilted his head toward Asher. "He's McConaughey."

"This isn't a fight I'm jumping into," Asher said as he studied the tower of bacon sitting in the center of the table. "How much bacon is that?"

"Twenty pounds," Sunnie replied as if it was perfectly normal to fry up the better part of a pig as a centerpiece. "But this is what you should really try." She picked up a toothpick holding a wedge of hot dog wrapped in bacon. "They're baked with brown sugar and to die for. And for dessert, we have—"

"Ice cream sundaes with bacon bits?" Teddy asked hopefully.

"No, but I suggested that, believe me. Fiona said ice cream and beer didn't mix." Sunnie rolled her eyes as if that statement was complete madness. "My mom made us chocolate-covered bacon instead."

Asher crossed his arms. "So, when Fiona said we were having an Anything Goes party, your first thought was bacon feast?"

Sunnie looked at him as if he'd sprouted an extra head. "Of course it was. After the Jasmine costume." She looked Asher up and down, shaking her head. "By the way, weak attempt, man."

Asher had been thinking too hard about what would happen *after* the party to consider the food and attire.

Teddy excused himself when Ryan arrived, and Sunnie went along to meet him. Owen grabbed a plate and started piling it with the bacon-wrapped hot dogs, four slices of bacon from the tower, a potato skin piled with bacon bits and bacon guacamole.

"Try as I may, I can't see anything wrong with this plate," Owen joked.

Asher conceded the victory to Sunnie. "Me, either."

"Are you guys ready to get this party started? We need to lay a base of liquor before the beer." Fiona appeared with a tray of tequila shots and a tub of cotton candy.

They'd been friends long enough that neither guy put up a fuss about the lack of limes and salt. Hell, she'd made Asher take so many of her sugar shots in the past, he was starting to like them.

They both took a glass and a pinch of the cotton candy. Fiona set down the tray and followed suit. They lifted their glasses.

"Here's to Anything Goes," Fiona said.

"Anything Goes," Asher repeated, watching her take the shot, the action drawing his gaze to her slender neck and the ample cleavage peeking out of the top of her dress.

A quick look to his left proved Owen was enjoying the view too.

Asher tried to beat down the flash of jealousy that flared.

He'd taken Teddy's advice and tried to work up a fantasy that included both Owen and Fiona. It hadn't gotten him as hot and hard as the one that starred him and Fiona alone. Or the one of him with Fiona and Sunnie. Or him, Fiona, Sunnie and Yvonne. He was only human, after all, but it wasn't completely out of the realm of—

Who was he kidding? His hard-on was raging when he imagined Fiona, but it deflated pretty quickly when Owen appeared in the dream scene.

"You should see the list of games Finn and Sunnie came up with. We'll be here until July if we play all of them. Want a beer?" she asked.

They went into the kitchen to grab a cold one from a huge tub of ice, then followed Fiona back to the living room. They socialized with her cousins and their friends as Finn and Sunnie took turns choosing the music.

Asher was relieved when Colm and Lochlan showed up, sans costumes as well. He hung out with them around the dining room table, eating enough bacon to choke a cat, until Sunnie declared everyone was there and it was time to play charades.

Charades was followed by Cards Against Humanity, which was followed by several drinking games, including flip cup relays, Kings, and something he'd never heard of called "Fuck You Pyramid." Several times throughout the evening, Asher had grabbed bottles of water for him, Fiona and Owen.

"More water?" she asked when he handed her the third bottle of the night. "Trying to keep me hydrated?"

"Or sober?" Owen interjected.

That's exactly what Asher was trying to do, but he wasn't going to admit it. "Considering we've done nothing but drink since we landed in Baltimore, I figure your body is crying out for H-two-O."

"You're probably right. Thursday almost did me in. Which is why I took it easy last night."

"You haven't had that much tonight, either." He pointed to Fiona's cup, perfectly aware that she'd been taking baby sips and nursing this last beer the better part of an hour.

"Trying to keep a clear head."

Asher wrapped his arm around her waist and pulled her closer. "Clear heads are good."

Owen didn't appear to agree as he set the water bottle down and chugged the rest of his beer. "Maybe," he said. "Maybe not."

Asher figured Owen's response was based on nerves.

"Hit the Quan" came on, and the game, which had been dying down, ended completely as several partiers started pushing the couch and chairs back to create a makeshift dance floor. Asher, Owen and Fiona joined the others in the line dance. Teddy boogied over near the end of the song.

"Where's Ryan?" Owen asked loudly, in order to be heard over the music.

Teddy merely shook his head and pointed his thumb toward the door. It looked like Ryan had been Tinder Strike Number Two.

Unlike with the Bulgarian bonbon, Teddy seemed to take Ryan's departure harder and he excused himself after a few more songs, claiming he was too tired from the previous two nights. Quite a few other people were starting to leave as well, so they didn't try to pressure him into staying, though Asher hated seeing the guy so down. Teddy was always the life of the party, so his early departure was out of character.

Asher worried he didn't leave because of Ryan, but because he didn't want to see what might happen after the party. Teddy wouldn't want to watch if everything imploded.

Colm headed up to his bedroom shortly after two, and it didn't take long for everyone else to disperse as well. Sunnie had passed out in her room an hour earlier, going too hard, too fast. He, Fiona, and Owen started tidying up the place until Asher looked around and realized they were the last three people still there.

"Wow." Fiona dropped down on the couch. "What a night."

"How many people are going to wake up tomorrow and think 'what the hell did I do'?" Owen asked with a chuckle, sitting next to her on the couch.

Asher claimed the other side, silently praying none of them fell into that category. "My guess is everyone who ate one of those gummy bears Leo brought. Way more than just sugar in those bad boys."

Fiona warmed up to his game. "Definitely Sunnie. Pretty sure she had no intention of making out with Finn's best friend, Landon. And I think Colm—if he remembers—is going to be horrified when he thinks about that dirty dancing he and Kelli were doing. They're not exactly friends when sober."

"Lochlan is probably going to regret the dent he made in the bacon tower," Asher added.

Fiona shook her head. "He's a gym nut. He'll have those calories worked off by noon tomorrow."

"That would explain the washboard abs," Owen grumbled. "It's almost enough to make me want to take my trainer more seriously. But not quite." The network was footing the bill for Owen's personal trainer, claiming they wanted to keep their hot star in shape, something Owen had never had to work too hard at in college, but was now having to make an effort at.

Asher laughed. "That's definitely the last time I play strip poker with him."

Fiona glanced down. "I have no idea where my bra is."

Owen snorted as he pointed to a pile of bras near the dining room table. "Over there. In the pretend bonfire. Does Yvonne always go full-on feminist when she's drunk?"

Fiona nodded. "When she's sober too. You just haven't been around her enough." She glanced at the pile. "Remind me to grab mine out of there later. That's my best strapless. Do you know how hard it is to find a strapless bra that holds the girls up just right?"

Asher shook his head. "Never considered it, but if you need some help holding the girls up right now…"

He reached over and she playfully swatted his hand away. Any other day, that type of teasing would have been followed by more, but it had the opposite effect tonight. Reminding them of why they were all still hanging around, why none of them had let themselves get too drunk.

Asher hadn't even started the Anything Goes portion of the night.

"Should we play another game?" Asher suggested.

Fiona and Owen groaned in unison. "No more alcohol," she pleaded.

"Not that kind of game. Truth or Dare."

She laughed. "Fancy reliving your first boy-girl middle school party?"

"Truth or dare, Owen?" Asher asked, not acknowledging her joke. He prayed Owen chose wisely. There was something Asher needed to see, needed to know before the night went any further.

Owen paused for just a second, then said, "Dare."

Asher took a deep breath and forced himself to issue the demand, even though he wasn't sure it was something he wanted to see. "Kiss Fee."

For all his hesitation and pregnant pauses all night, Owen didn't waver this time. He simply reached over, cupped Fiona's cheek to turn her face to his and kissed her. It reminded Asher of the steamy, openmouthed liplock he'd laid on her under the mistletoe.

When they parted, Fiona turned to look over her shoulder at him. He schooled his features because he didn't want her to see anything that wasn't there. Or anything that was. Like the spark of jealousy that told him tonight was going to be tough.

Owen had been right. They would have been smarter to drink more.

"Your turn, Owen," Asher said, his eyes still locked with Fiona's.

"Truth or dare, Fee."

She licked her lips as she faced Owen once more. "Truth."

Owen chuckled. "Chicken shit."

She grinned but didn't bother to deny it.

"Are you okay with this?" Owen asked.

Fiona blew out a long breath. "Should have taken the dare."

"Tell me," Owen repeated. Asher was grateful to his friend because he had the presence of mind to do what Asher had failed to do. Make sure Fiona was on board.

It took her a few seconds to reply and when she did, it was merely a nod.

"No," Asher said, reaching out to take her hand in his. "Say the words, Fiona. Are you okay with what we want to happen here tonight?"

"It's Anything Goes night. I thought we weren't supposed to think about it or talk about it. Just go with what we want."

"So we're cheating," Asher said. "Is this what you want?"

She nodded again. "Yes," she whispered. "Truth or dare, Ash?"

"Dare," he replied.

"Kiss me." Then she held up her hand to stop him when he leaned toward her. "A real kiss. Longer than ten seconds. Mouths open. Tongues."

Owen covered his mouth to hide the grin her demands produced. "In other words," he added, "she doesn't want a repeat of that weak-assed attempt you made the other night."

"Laugh it up," Asher said. "I'm perfectly aware of how to kiss a woman."

He reached out and took her face in his hands, leaning forward to give Fiona the kiss he'd dreamed of for years…ever since he'd been that awkward, shy eighteen-year-old boy.

Fiona's hands gripped his shoulders as he pressed her lips apart with his. He dipped his tongue in, the two of them snickering as they were assaulted by the taste of bacon. "Delicious," he murmured just before he resumed the kiss. He reached for her hair, twisting the long strands around his fingers, tugging, slowly applying pressure until she gasped. Then he released her hair, his knuckles brushing her cheeks. She whimpered softly when he ran his fingertips over her neck and along the top of her dress, touching the silky skin at the top of her breasts.

Fiona pulled away first.

"Jesus, that was hot," Owen muttered, prompting her to look over her shoulder at him.

Fiona's gaze returned to Asher's. "Truth or dare?"

"You just had your turn," Asher replied.

At the same time, Owen said, "Who are you asking?"

"Both of you. Truth or dare?"

Asher glanced at Owen as they said in unison, "Dare."

"Take me to the bedroom."

Chapter Seven

Fiona fought down the butterflies in her stomach as they crossed the threshold to her bedroom.

"That's problematic," Owen said as the three of them faced the two single beds on opposite walls.

"Should have thought that through," she said. "I mean…actually, I did earlier, but then I smelled the bacon frying and got distracted."

"Good to know where we stand as far as the pecking order. After bacon. Duly noted," Asher joked, prompting Fiona to laugh with him.

Owen was the only one who didn't laugh. Instead, he locked gazes with Asher. "So, what's next?"

It occurred to Fiona that Asher and Owen hadn't discussed what was going to happen. Which made sense when she considered Asher's demand that Anything Goes be instinctive, but stupid on every other level. She'd made the comment to her cousins that Asher and Owen didn't really strike her as threesome kind of guys, and seeing Owen's reticence now only solidified that belief.

Fiona opened her mouth, ready to let them both off the hook. It would kill her to sleep alone tonight because she hadn't been kidding about her dry spell. At least she wasn't sharing this room with any of her cousins. She could whip out her newest vibrator—the thruster. That bad boy had three speeds, seven functions, a clit stimulator and some serious girth. Happy Clam clenched at the thought of it.

So maybe it *wouldn't* kill her to sleep alone.

Asher stepped behind her, embracing her as she rested against his chest. She'd never noticed how…hard…Asher was. And not just below the waist, though there was a telltale bulge brushing against her ass that told her he was hard all over.

What she hadn't realized was how strong, how built he was. It wasn't that he was a slouch. She knew he worked out, and on rare occasions, he'd joined her for a jog and had more than held his own. The difference was in the way he was holding her now. In the past, his hugs had been either friendly or comforting, softer, like a pillow she could sink into. This embrace was different. It was iron and steel, and there was a certain strength that spoke of possession, of passion.

It was hot.

She revised her previous opinion, back to believing it *would* kill her to sleep alone…vibrator or not.

Asher's hands drifted up until he was cupping her breasts. Owen's gaze followed his movements and a quick peek told Fiona that while both men might be a little bit reserved, it wasn't impacting their arousal. Owen's hard-on was apparent beneath his jeans.

Her face must have given away her current opinion on Operation Ménage a Trois because Owen smiled. Then he moved in front of her, leaned down and kissed her.

She was transported back in time to sophomore year. His kisses were just as sweet, just as gentle as they'd been back then.

And they were a far cry from Asher's. His kiss on the couch… Holy fuck. It had hit every hot button in her body all at the same time.

Asher remained behind her as she and Owen kissed, but that didn't mean she wasn't completely aware of every move he made. He was still cupping her breasts, the silk of her ball gown a barrier. Not that it mattered. Everything Asher did packed a punch. His light cupping soon turned to something more as he tightened his grip, plumping the flesh in a way that had her going light-headed.

She broke the kiss with Owen for a split second, desperate to draw in some much-needed air. He reached up, taking her face in his hands, pulling her lips back to his, greedily.

Asher's hands disappeared, but Owen didn't give her a chance to complain about it. When she felt Asher searching for the zipper at the back of her dress, the protest died anyway.

Fiona liked sex—a lot—but her list of lovers was pretty short. She'd lost her virginity to the nephew of her parents' drummer, in a relationship that could only be described as summer love. The handsome boy had joined them on the bus during his holiday from school, and she'd fallen head over ass as only a seventeen-year-old girl can do. It ended when September came. Then there'd been an unfortunate one-night stand her freshman year in college that she blamed on too much alcohol. Then Owen. Then Brock.

Four lovers.

If she didn't include the countless sex toys stashed under her bed at home. Teddy had found the box once—nosy fucker—and acted like she was some sort of sex maniac. Told her she could open up a sex shop with her inventory.

Fiona sucked in a deep breath as the silence in the room was filled with the sound of Asher sliding the zipper down. Owen pulled away, his eyes drifting lower.

She tilted her head and gave him a sassy grin. "*Now* you stop kissing me?"

He winked at her. "Making sure I've got a good spot for the show."

"You've seen it all before," she reminded him.

Owen never bothered to look at her face. "I was young and stupid and too worried about getting my rocks off to pay attention to the finer details."

Asher released his hold on the zipper tab, and the entire dress simply fell to the floor. She'd tugged off her bra for Yvonne's fake bonfire earlier, which left her in just a thong.

Up until that moment, everything had felt…easy. Controllable.

But now that she was standing in front of her completely dressed best friends, almost totally naked, a kernel of unease slipped in. Ordinarily, Fiona's self-confidence was firmly in place, a staple that never faltered. Ailis had told her once that it might be easier if she actually toned back her convictions, her belief in herself and her abilities, but Fiona was smart enough to understand that only made things easier for other people, not her.

Now, however, for one of the few times in her life, she was struggling to stand with poise without worrying what they thought.

Well, not Owen so much. He was a bit like a loveable puppy dog who operated solely on pure adoration. She could see it now as his gaze raked her from head to toe, his expression one of appreciation. Something he backed up with a wolf whistle.

"You're still the hottest girl on the planet."

She giggled, wishing those words would sink in, would dim the flutter in her belly, but they didn't. Because Asher was behind her, and she couldn't see his face, couldn't tell…

"Turn around, Fee."

God, when had Asher's voice gotten so grumbly and deep and sexy as fuck?

She took a deep breath, then twisted to face him.

Unlike Owen, his expressions were harder to read. There was no denying the hunger, the desire she saw there, but she needed him to say something. Anything.

She didn't realize she was holding her breath until his eyes met hers.

He didn't say a word. He didn't have to. One look said it all.

She licked her lips, her lungs burning from a lack of air.

When did she forget how to breathe?

Asher saved her. He pressed his lips to hers and she realized air wasn't necessary. All she needed in that moment, in that place and time, was him. To hell with the rest.

She started slightly when Owen took over Asher's role, stepping behind her. His hands landed on her hips briefly before they started to roam, over her waist, then down to the bare globes of her ass. He caressed and squeezed and touched. Owen's finger traced the line of her thong from where it began low on her hips until it disappeared between the slit of her thighs.

Through it all, Asher kissed her. No, he devoured her—with his tongue, his teeth, his lips. His hands gripped her face, turning her slightly whenever he wanted to deepen the kiss even more.

When his fingers curled into fists, grasping her hair, she moaned into his mouth. The sound must have spurred him on, because the grip tightened and he pulled. Hard.

Her scalp burned, then tingled, but Fiona didn't seek freedom. Her hands rested on his chest before she moved them up to his face, using the single drop of strength she had left to push his mouth away from hers just long enough to say, "Harder."

It was Asher's turn to groan. He gave her what she wanted, but there was something in his eyes that told him she was getting her way because it was what *he* desired.

Fiona was taken aback by the beast she'd unleashed.

Her costume suddenly seemed perfect.

Fiona struggled to assimilate this intense, demanding alpha male with her affable, sweet friend. The crazy part was…this side of Asher had always been there, so her shock seemed misplaced.

He'd always taken charge of the writing team, keeping them on track, guiding them through dry spells, speaking on their behalf to the producers and director. But he always tempered the strength and made it seem less threatening, which, in turn, made him the perfect spokesperson. Everyone genuinely liked Asher, but no one would ever call him a pushover.

Asher broke off the kiss, his eyes never leaving her face, even as he spoke to Owen.

"Grab the comforters from the bed, Owen. Put them on the floor."

She felt a chill as cold air hit her back at Owen's disappearance. She'd been so snug between them she'd felt almost feverish.

Asher pulled her hair again, but this time he wasn't kissing her. He was watching her.

Her eyes drifted closed and she shuddered.

"Why does that feel so good? It should hurt."

Asher didn't answer. Instead, he leaned closer and placed a soft kiss on her cheek. The gentle gesture worked as a counterpoint to his rougher touches.

Everything he did felt like it was a contradiction.

"Asher."

Asher released her and they both looked toward Owen, who'd built them a cozy nest in the center of the floor with all the comforters, blankets and pillows in the room.

Once again, Fiona felt overwhelmed. Standing naked in front of them was one thing, watching them undress and then lying down between them was another.

Her opinion of her aunts Lily and Lauren rose several notches.

A quick glance at Owen proved he was having the same thoughts. Like her, Owen wasn't lacking in the confidence department, but there was no mistaking the uncertainty on his face.

She offered him the same encouragement he'd given her. She winked.

He chuckled, then reached for the hem of his T-shirt, tugging it over his head.

Damn. That might have been too much encouragement. Her heart started to race—with nervousness and excitement.

A shirtless Owen wasn't an unusual site, but that didn't soften the impact. The guy was ripped, like movie-star ripped, like PhotoShopped ripped, like—

"You got a little drool right there, Fee," Owen said, pointing to the side of his mouth.

Before she could come up with some witty rejoinder, Asher chuckled and walked toward their makeshift bed on the floor. He began to unbutton his shirt, and every smart-ass thing she wanted to say flew out of her head.

Fiona's gaze was glued on his fingers as, button by button, he revealed more of his chest. She wondered if they could hear her heart pounding because it was deafening her.

Asher shrugged his shirt off and tossed it toward her bed, then he took his glasses off and set them on the nightstand.

So long Clark Kent. Hello Superman.

The three of them stood there for a moment, a silent standoff. Fiona's mind was whirling, touching on a thousand different things in a split second.

Her brain whizzed around like the pieces on a Candy Land board. She landed at Holy Hotness Times Two Town, traveled through What the Hell Am I Doing Grove, boogied across the How the Fuck Does This Work Bridge and finally drew a What Now card.

"So…what's next?" They were the same words Owen had used earlier, and now she knew why. It was the only thing she could think to say.

Asher smiled and held his hand out to her. "Come here, Fiona."

Her feet started moving before her brain. She walked over to him, then let him hold her hand as she knelt on top of the comforters. Asher followed her down, the two of them sitting beside each other. Owen was slower to join them, not moving until they both looked up at him.

And suddenly she was struck by the sense that he wasn't as all-in as she'd thought.

That concern was eased when Owen knelt, then reached out to take her hand, squeezing it before raising it to his mouth and kissing the tips of her fingers. Using his grip on her hand, he pulled it across his chest, over his nipples, along the tight plane of his stomach.

"Lay down." Asher's request—no, he was using the power voice again, which made it a demand—distracted her.

Oh shit.

Moment of truth.

She licked her lips but all the moisture in her mouth had completely evaporated. When had this shifted from exciting to terrifying?

Before she could consider that or act on Asher's command, Owen cupped her face to turn it toward him. He kissed her, and she tried to let the sweetness of it soothe her, calm her down.

Unfortunately, it didn't work—and panic started to set in.

This wasn't right.

Was it?

She turned her head away, her eyes connecting with Asher's.

He took one look at her face and frowned. "Wait," he said, when Owen made a move to resume their kiss.

Owen stilled, then looked at her. *Really* looked at her. "Fee?"

"Can we take a second?" she asked, feeling foolish. She'd been the one to invite them to her bedroom. She'd given them the green light.

Asher reached for her hand, his fingers caressing it, his thumb massaging her palm in a surprisingly soothing way. "We can take as long as you need," Asher said, placing a soft kiss on her cheek. "We can also stop."

"No," she said quickly. "I just need to catch up and…" She blew out a long breath. "This is sort of intimidating. I mean, there's one of me and two of…" Fiona pointed toward their crotches and both men laughed.

She narrowed her eyes, though she wasn't really mad. "I mean it. Happy Clam is the only entrance down there, as far as she's concerned, and I have to respect her feelings on that matter. Which leaves us with one lightsaber dangling while—"

"I wouldn't say dangling," Owen interrupted, wiggling his eyebrows at her.

She laughed—and her sudden attack of nerves vanished just like that.

No matter what happened tonight, these guys were always going to be her friends.

The second the truth of that sank in, everything that was freaking her out faded away. She was being silly, overreacting. Owen and Asher cared about her. They could make this work.

Maybe.

"Well, they do say two heads are better than one," she joked, trying to distract them from her momentary lapse.

Owen cracked up, but Asher, typical lovely man, wouldn't let her moment of panic slide by so easily.

"No sex tonight," Asher said.

"Wait." Now that she'd turned a corner, she didn't want them to make any hasty decisions.

"No. I'm serious," Asher insisted. "We'll fool around, make out, test some boundaries. Owen and I will leave our pants on. If this still feels right in the morning, we'll go all the way. Okay?"

Owen didn't hesitate to agree. "Sounds like a good idea."

Fiona tilted her head, wishing she weren't so relieved. That response seemed pretty telling. "What about your lightsaber?"

Owen made a sound she assumed was meant to be him turning off the weapon. "*Schoom.*"

"It's that easy?" she asked, feeling a wee bit guilty for putting the brakes on so suddenly.

He shook his head. "I wish. But some things are worth waiting for."

Leave it to her oaf of a friend to find the perfect thing to say.

"Come on. Let's all lay down," Asher suggested.

They moved as a unit and now that sex was off the table, Fiona could simply enjoy the moment, the closeness, the warmth.

She lay on her back and both men turned to face her. Owen kissed her as Asher played with her breasts, then bent his head to suck one of her nipples into his mouth.

Fiona placed a hand on the back of each of their heads, running her fingers through their hair, taking time to study their differences. Owen's hair was longer and softer, while Asher's was much thicker.

That was as far as her studies took her before Asher playfully sank his teeth into her sensitive nipple, just hard enough to provoke a gasp.

Owen studied her face before looking down. "Take it easy on her, Ash."

"I'm fine," she hastened to say, afraid Asher would take Owen's suggestion to heart.

Owen gave her a crooked grin. "Kinky girl."

She snorted. "I wish."

Their conversation ended there—because Asher bit harder.

Her back arched involuntarily, the action like a mallet against the knee.

"God!" she cried out. "That's so…" A million words floated through her brain. Teddy called her the Queen of Vocabulary, and she was almost sorry he wasn't there to hear this list. It was a doozy.

Incredible. Stimulating. Intense. Amazing. Mind-blowing. Spectacular. Astonishing. Fucktastic.

Finally, she just landed on the easiest one to say. "Hot."

"We're just getting started," Asher murmured.

She sucked in a loud breath when he reached down, his fingers sliding under the elastic of her thong. He wasted no time finding her clit, pressing and rubbing until she saw honest-to-God stars.

"Asher." His name came out with a gasp.

"That's right, Fee. Say my name. Let me hear you scream it when you come."

Chapter Eight

Asher wanted to kick his own ass the second he'd suggested no sex. Not because it wasn't the right thing to do, but because it was going to leave him in some serious physical pain later on. Blue balls weren't a good thing. Ever.

Regardless, he would deal with it because he wasn't going to screw up this chance with Fiona.

And Owen.

Asher had to keep remembering that Owen was a part of this too.

He'd like to say having his best friend in the room with them was a turn-on, but it wasn't. However, it wasn't a buzzkill, either. It was just…different. Something that would take some getting used to.

He hoped he got used to it.

The twinges of jealousy he felt watching Owen as he kissed her or touched her were still there, but it was getting easier to push the feeling away.

Okay. It wasn't easier, but he'd get there. He had to. He was as committed to protecting his friendship with Owen as he was to claiming Fiona's heart.

And it wasn't like his sex life hadn't been one big experiment in exploration anyway. Christina Saunders hadn't only been his Creative Writing teacher, she'd been his instructor in the bedroom as well. She'd exposed him to tantric sex, guided him through most of the positions in the *Kama Sutra*, and as a member of a local sex club, she'd enrolled them in classes on shibari and wax play.

The more he learned, the more his dominant side began to emerge—a fact that delighted Christina as much as it bothered her.

She enjoyed his dominance in the bedroom—on occasion—but it wasn't something Asher could turn on and off. And that was when they'd both realized the pupil had outgrown the teacher.

Unfortunately, he and Christina had never brought another person to the bed, never included another man—or woman—in their play. So he was going to have to figure this one out on his own.

Owen stopped playing with her breasts, his gaze glued to where Asher's hand had slipped beneath Fiona's thong.

She was absolutely beautiful, Asher's idea of feminine perfection, though he knew there were parts of herself that she viewed as anything less than ideal. Her plump, full breasts fit his hand perfectly, while her figure was more straight than hourglass. She sometimes mentioned her longing for curves. Every time she did, he'd reminded her she was jogging them off. He wasn't wrong. Her legs were lean, slim, muscular, and he'd give a million dollars right now to have them wrapped around his waist. Or his shoulders.

"Grab her wrists, Owen. Hold them above her head."

Owen didn't hesitate to do as asked. Asher dreamed of tying Fiona to his headboard, of keeping her on the edge of a climax for hours while he—fuck, *they*—played with her. She liked it when he pulled her hair. It gave him hope that she'd like to try other, kinkier things.

Fiona was a true Collins, a grab-life-by-the-horns type of girl. In truth, it wasn't *her* penchant for bedroom adventures he was worried about.

It was Owen's.

His friend had one wrist in each hand, sort of awkwardly holding them up. The position meant he was blocking Fiona's view of what Asher was doing.

He knelt up, gesturing for Owen to release her. Asher grasped her arms, crisscrossing her wrists above her head so he could hold her in place with just one hand. He demonstrated for Owen.

"This way." Asher reached down with his free hand and pinched one of Fiona's nipples. She gasped, then moaned. "So you can still play with her."

Owen nodded that he understood and Asher released her, letting Owen take over. Shifting back between her legs, Asher tugged off her thong.

"Open your legs, princess."

She did as he said without comment or delay. Asher took a second to study her face. Her cheeks were flushed, and there was no denying she liked the idea of being held down, captured. He'd tried to initiate a capture fantasy with Christina one night, but she'd lost her shit, then spent the next two hours guiding him through feminist literature and trying to convince him his desires were wrong. The night ended with him binding her in shibari rope, withholding her orgasm until she'd admitted *she* was wrong. It was one of the hottest, most sexually charged nights of their relationship.

It was also the beginning of the end, the moment they both realized the writing on the wall had changed.

Asher lifted Fiona's legs, tugging her knees over his shoulders just as he desired, and he bent down to place a kiss on her clit. He'd anticipated Fiona's hip-jerking reaction, so his hand was pressed firmly on her stomach, holding her to the floor.

He upped the ante, sucking her clit into his mouth, then nipping at the distended flesh with his teeth. Through it all, she struggled to move, to drive her pussy closer to his mouth, trying to grab more.

"God, Ash…"

He glanced up, wanting to see her face, but his eyes met Owen's. Owen still held her wrists, his free hand lazily caressing her breasts. Clearly, he was too distracted by what Asher was doing to concentrate on his own actions.

"Suck on her breast. Play with the nipple." Asher had just gotten out of a relationship because he was tired of playing the student. He really didn't want to get into one where he took on the role of teacher.

Owen responded, his head lowering to take her nipple into his mouth. Fiona sighed, Owen's touch decidedly gentler than his, if her almost-relaxed reaction was anything to judge by.

Asher took a deep breath and pushed his wayward thoughts away. It was only their first night. They had all the time in the world to learn each other's hot buttons, to explore and grow.

He took her clit back into his mouth as he slid two fingers inside her.

"Yes," Fiona hissed when he drove deep, pumping in and out several times. She was wet, her pussy on fire, and once again, he cursed himself for promising no sex. He wanted to be inside her, wanted to lose himself in all that heat, let her burn him, scorch him.

Fiona started to tremble, her inner muscles clenching against his fingers. She was close.

He withdrew before she could get there.

"No! Wait," she cried out.

He shook his head as he rose, kneeling between her legs. "No. *You're* going to wait."

Her forehead creased briefly with confusion before her eyes flashed with irritation. "Asher. Be a good boy and put your fingers back inside me."

He laughed. "Oh, princess. That's never going to work with me."

And then, because she had the devil in her, Fiona flashed her bright baby blues at Owen. "Owen, sweetie, you're nice than Asher. Everyone knows that. Knock that meanie out of the way and take over down there."

Owen, the asshole, actually looked like he was considering it.

"Don't let go of her hands, Owen."

Owen's grip tightened—and for the first time, Fiona actually struggled against it.

"I don't know what game you're playing, but I was close, Ash. Like, *really* close. Painfully close."

"If you want it quick and merely satisfying, say the word. Owen and I can leave and you can grab your vibrator. If you want to take your time, let it build while we kiss, lick, suck and bite every inch of you until you explode in our arms, we're doing this my way."

Fiona stopped trying to free her hands from Owen's grip.

"Damn, man," Owen murmured. "That sounds fucking hot."

Asher grinned, but Fiona didn't. Instead, she was nibbling on her lower lip and, for a second, he thought she was actually trying to decide which route to go.

"Seriously?" Owen muttered. "The answer isn't obvious?"

She shot him a dirty look. "It is. I'm just…I'm not used to denying myself. Anything, really. Food, shoes, purses, orgasms. If I want it, I get it."

Asher nodded solemnly. "I know. You're spoiled."

She scowled. "Not because I make other people buy everything for me. I work damn hard for my salary, which happens to be a great one."

"And your parents are richer than God," Owen added.

"Fuck you, Owen."

The three of them cracked up as Asher lay back down beside Fiona, and Owen released her hands. Fiona sighed, clearly thinking they were taking a breather.

Asher had other plans in mind. He liked keeping her off-balance, on guard, for the very reasons she'd just stated. Fiona lived a life of self-gratification, and it was becoming pretty obvious Brock had simply given her whatever she wanted in bed without challenging her, pushing her limits.

Reaching down, Asher unbuckled his belt, sliding it from the loops, allowing the *whishing* sound to fill the silence.

Fiona's eyes followed the movement of his hands as he sat up and reached for her wrists once more.

"Wait," she said.

"I can use the belt to bind your hands or to spank your ass. Don't tell me to wait one more time. If you don't like something I'm doing, tell me no and I'll stop. Always. But if it's something you want, don't pretend you don't."

"Wow," she said.

He tilted his head. "Wow what?"

Fiona opened her mouth, but no sound came out, so Owen answered the question. "You are one scary fucker. And I'm pretty sure Fiona's as turned on by it as I am."

Asher expected Fiona to either laugh or correct him, but instead she merely nodded. "You come off as so nice when you're Clark Kent. Then boom, Sexy Superman."

He couldn't resist her a second longer, so he gave her a kiss. He'd meant to keep it quick, mouths closed, but Fiona wasn't finished fighting yet. She wrapped her arms around his neck and opened her lips, her tongue seeking his. He let her guide the kiss because he was nobody's fool. He loved kissing her.

When they parted, he unclasped her hands from behind his neck and tugged them upwards again, twisting the leather around her wrists and tying it off.

"Not your first time doing that," Owen said softly.

It wasn't a question, so Asher didn't bother to answer. The proof was in the efficient knot anyway.

"Leave your hands above your head, Fee." He didn't say "or else," but from the way she shivered slightly, he knew it had been implied.

Asher lowered his head to Fiona's breast, gripping the flesh firmly. He shot a quick glance at Owen, indicating he should hop in and play with the other.

Hopefully, once the shock of what they were doing wore off, Owen wouldn't keep reverting to spectator.

Together, they each played with her breasts. Asher would occasionally catch a glimpse of what Owen was doing, and he got a sense his friend was actually mimicking him, following his lead.

Fiona wriggled beneath them, her soft cries, her moans telling him when he'd done something she liked.

Asher deepened the suction on her nipple, keeping it in his mouth, as his hand slid lower, the back of his knuckles brushing along her stomach until he reached her pussy.

Fiona's legs were clenched as she rubbed her thighs together. She was desperate for stimulation and failing to find enough on her own.

The second she felt his fingers near her clit, her legs fell apart, inviting him to play.

Asher raised his head, his gaze on Owen, capturing his friend's attention.

"Want to touch her?" Asher asked.

Owen nodded, his own hand caressing Fiona as it drifted lower. He paused when his hand rested by Asher's.

Asher was perfectly capable of taking the reins, of telling Owen what to do. But was Owen okay with that? It wasn't like this was Owen's first time with a woman. Hell, it wasn't even his first time with Fiona. So why all the hesitance?

"Touch her," Asher whispered, when Owen made no further movement.

Owen's finger grazed her clit. Fiona jerked at the sudden touch but didn't make a sound. Owen was too gentle—in everything.

Asher gave up trying to be a team player. "Like this." He put his hand on top of Owen's and applied pressure, his finger pushing Owen's against her clit.

That time, Fiona responded with a loud, "yes," and Owen grinned.

"Rub it. Fast and hard. But don't let her come."

Owen frowned. "How will I know if—"

"Pay attention. Listen to her. Feel what her body is saying."

Fiona's neck arched. "Stop. Talking," she groaned. "More."

As Owen stroked her clit, Asher took advantage of other areas. He pushed two fingers back inside her, matching his thrusts to Owen's motion.

Fiona's hips lifted and fell and once again, Asher was overcome with the need to unzip his pants and take her.

He thought the only thing stopping him was that they'd agreed to take sex off the table, but Asher forced himself to admit the truth.

He didn't want Owen there when he made love to Fiona.

"Fuck."

He hadn't meant to say the word aloud. Fortunately, neither Owen nor even Miss Tone Fiona realized it was frustration, not arousal behind it.

Once more he felt her reaching the peak, so he withdrew his fingers, letting one wet digit drift lower, wiggling it around her anus.

"Asher," Fiona cried out, her reaction in direct opposition to her earlier comment about anal play.

She liked it. He knew she would.

Owen glanced down and realized what he was doing.

"She's going to kill you," Owen muttered, "the second she stops coming."

Asher grinned, then pressed the tip of his index finger into the tight ring of flesh. He wouldn't do more than that tonight, but he definitely wanted to give Fiona something to think about for next time.

For the first time all night, Owen took some initiative and pushed his own fingers inside her pussy. Asher was impressed when his friend even managed to keep the pressure on her clit by using his thumb.

It didn't take more than a few thrusts before Fiona went up and over, her body shuddering with her climax. Her cheeks were flushed, her eyes closed as she trembled. He loved the little sounds she made—the perfect blend of surprise mingled with mews of pleasure. Neither Owen nor Asher stopped touching her, stroking her, as wave after wave passed through her, and she cried out, "Holy fuck! God. Jesus."

Asher had promised her an explosion. Looked like he—they—had managed it.

When she landed, Owen was the first to withdraw, leaning over to give her a soft kiss.

Fiona gave him a drowsy smile.

"Going to the bathroom," he said. "Need a few minutes alone with my lightsaber."

She frowned. "Owen, wait. I know we said—"

"No, Fee," Owen interrupted her. "It's better this way. We'll talk about it in the morning."

She nodded slowly as Owen pushed himself up from the floor. Asher noticed his friend never looked in his direction as he walked out of the room.

So, Owen felt the same way.

This time, Asher managed to keep the *fuck* inside his head. He crawled alongside Fiona, reaching up to free her hands.

"Bondage, huh? That was a surprise," she said saucily.

Despite the tightness in his chest that told him things were going to take a bad turn really soon, he laughed. "That's just one surprise."

Once she was free, she tugged him toward her.

"I should wash my hands, Fee."

"In a minute." She pulled his head down toward hers and kissed him. Though she initiated it, he took over, deepening the connection, wishing there was an easy solution to all of this.

Because kissing Fiona was the closest he'd ever been to heaven…and Asher really didn't want to leave paradise.

Chapter Nine

The sky was only just starting to brighten the room when Fiona felt something tapping the bottom of her foot.

She blinked, trying to make the room come into focus. That was when she felt the first twinges of some serious stiffness. Sleeping on the floor sucked.

What didn't suck was waking up naked between two super-hot guys.

That was when she felt the tap on her foot again—and she realized Teddy was standing in her room, looking down at them.

She tugged the blanket higher, concealing her nakedness.

Teddy jerked his head toward the living room.

She nodded, then waited as he left the room before carefully shimmying out of their makeshift nest. It wasn't that hard, really. Owen had rolled over, his back to her.

All she had to do was gently move Asher's hand from her stomach and push herself up and out. She tiptoed to the hook on the back of her bedroom door and grabbed her terry cloth robe, shrugging it on before heading to the living room.

A glance at the clock told her it was six a.m. She, Owen and Asher had turned off the light and gone to sleep shortly after three thirty.

Teddy was standing by the coffee table. The room was wrecked, which only drove home how badly she wanted to crawl back into the nest she'd just left and sleep for the next four days.

"What the hell, Teddy? How did you get in here?"

"Riley was already in the kitchen, cooking for the breakfast shift, so she let me in the back door. I couldn't sleep."

"That's fascinating. I could. I was."

"So?"

"So?" she asked. "Please tell me you didn't walk over here predawn, just to wake me up to get the details of my night."

"There are details?"

Fiona blew out a long, frustrated breath. She'd been friends with Teddy long enough to know he wouldn't leave until she gave him what he wanted.

Then she realized he was here because he knew her too. Knew she would need a chance to debrief, to discuss what had happened. Sometimes it felt as if the two of them shared some sort of mental connection, like twins, where one of them always knew when the other was hurting or needed to talk.

"We didn't have sex." She felt like that was the most important detail.

"But?" he prompted.

"We did a hell of a lot else."

"And?"

"And it was amazing, but…"

"But?"

"Dammit, Teddy. I've had too much to drink this week and precious little sleep. Please don't ask me for answers. I don't have any."

"Yeah. I can see that. So, let's start small. What's 'a hell of a lot else'?" he asked after a brief pause.

"Seriously?"

"Maybe you'll figure out the big stuff if you analyze the good stuff."

"I'm not going into details."

"Give me one detail then. One juicy one."

Fiona was frustrated by the whole conversation. When Teddy didn't say anything else, she raised her hand and waved it around, clueless to what he might want to hear. "Like what?"

"How far did you go with Asher?"

Fiona wasn't sure how to answer that. She'd always thought Teddy's teasing about Asher turning gay was just that—a joke. If she found out that Teddy was in love with Asher, she'd move to fucking China. This triangle was already a hot mess. She wasn't looking to turn it into a square.

"Why?"

"Did he take off his clothes?"

Fiona took the bait. "Just his shirt."

"Did your hand linger below the waist?"

She shook her head. "No. We took sex off the table pretty early on. Instead, they just touched and kissed me and…" *Made me come so hard I thought my head was going to pop off.*

"Wow. That's some blush. And you didn't even get a gander at the good stuff."

"What am I missing?"

Teddy plopped down on the couch with a chuckle. "You already know."

She sat next to him, shaking her head. "No, I don't."

Teddy tilted his head. "Biggus Dickus."

On their list of long-running jokes, Biggus Dickus ranked right up there with Teddy trying to convert Asher to homosexuality. "That's a joke."

"All jokes are based in reality."

It was something they said all the time. Because of that, she'd always sort of wondered...okay...fantasized about Asher's dick. Curious to see it. To feel it.

Too many times they'd find the humor in something that was very real and probably not funny, but they were all firm believers that if you didn't laugh, you'd cry.

"Asher's packing some serious heat."

She grinned. "That doesn't sound like a bad thing. What are we talking about here? Inches? Girth?"

"Both. Why do you think I keep trying to bring him over to my team? It's pretty fucking impressive. Sort of a challenge, you know?"

Fiona closed her eyes, rubbing her temple. She threw her legs over Teddy's lap and he pulled her closer. Teddy was the greatest hugger in the world, and right now, she needed one. She was feeling confused and stressed.

"Did you seriously come over here to talk about Asher's dick?"

Teddy shook his head. "No. I've been lying in that damn bed for hours wondering what was going on with the three of you, and finally I just gave in and came over to see."

"You don't approve of this, do you?"

"It's not my place to say."

Fiona wasn't sure she agreed with that. Last night might have been a threesome, but after so many years of close friendship, of functioning as a unit of four, she sort of thought Teddy did deserve some say. Because what happened next didn't just affect her, Owen, and Asher, it impacted Teddy's life as well.

"Say it anyway," she urged.

"It's not a case of approval. I'm not sure it will work. Too many factors at play and none of you has access to the whole picture. You're all looking at each other through foggy glass."

Fiona didn't have a clue what that meant. "I hate this feeling, Teddy. I've always been this 'see what you want and go get it' girl. And I nail it…in every aspect of life. Except romance. The second my heart becomes engaged, I fuck everything up."

"Maybe you fuck it up *because* of that personality trait. You know what you want from a relationship, Fee. You always have. You just approach it the wrong way, trying to twist the man into your image of true love instead of finding the person who falls into that role naturally."

She hadn't considered that. "Owen and Asher…" She didn't know how to finish the sentence the second she started it.

"You in love with both of them?" he asked. "Does it feel like something the three of you could make a run at?"

"Honestly?" She shook her head. "No."

Her response didn't just take Teddy by surprise, but her too. "Wait. What? Seriously?"

"I wanted to try because it seemed like the easy answer."

Teddy chuckled. "You realize that's a ridiculous outlook, right? I mean, who approaches the problem of which guy to date with the thought, 'Oooo…ménage. That'll be easy.'"

She rolled her eyes. "My family."

"Fuck. Yeah. Point to you."

"What am I going to do, Teddy?"

"Pick the right one."

She put her head back on his shoulder but didn't respond.

"You know who you want, don't you?"

She nodded.

"Want to give me a hint?"

Fiona lifted her head. "I can't. I need to talk to—" She paused, stopping short of saying the name. "Do you think this is going to ruin things? Mess up the friendship?"

Teddy considered that, then shrugged. "I don't know, Fee. I hope not."

***

The second time Fiona woke up, she rolled over, stretched, and glanced at the clock. It was almost noon. She and Teddy had hung out on the couch for nearly an hour, talking very little, both lost in their thoughts. When she started to drift off, Teddy shook her, told her to go back to her room and then left, heading back to the hotel. The dark circles under his eyes proved he hadn't lied about struggling to sleep. She hoped he'd managed to grab some after he left.

Glancing over her shoulder, she saw Asher still sound asleep on the floor next to her. Her body ached. After Teddy left, she'd been tempted to crawl into the bed, but that didn't seem fair to the guys. Next time, they were pushing the beds together.

Her heart clenched. Once she told them her feelings, there wouldn't be a next time.

That was when she realized Owen was missing.

She sat up slowly, careful not to wake Asher. Pulling on her robe once more, she knotted the tie around her waist and went in search of Owen.

He was sitting alone on the couch texting someone, fully dressed and clearly waiting for them to wake up.

"Hey, you," she said, joining him.

Owen smiled, reaching out to take one of her hands in his. "Hey, yourself. Feeling okay this morning?"

"Stiff. Sleeping on the floor is for teenagers."

"You can say that again."

"What are you doing out here all by yourself? You should have woken me up."

Owen sighed. "You both looked too peaceful."

Fiona struggled for what to say next. For someone who made a living with words, they were failing her here. Owen seemed to be suffering the same loss.

"So," he said at last. "Asher was a surprise."

She grabbed the subject and ran with it. "I know. Who the hell was that guy? He's so easygoing and friendly most of the time. Then you put him in bed and boom, he pulls out that gruff, deep, sexy voice."

"Yeah. He was…wow. No offense," he hastened to add. "I mean obviously I was mainly focused on you."

She laughed. "No offense taken. Believe me."

"Fee, I—"

"Owen, listen—"

They both stopped short when they spoke at the same time.

"You go ahead," she said, cowardly trying to put off saying what needed to be said.

"I got the audition."

Thoughts of the previous night flew out of her head. "Oh my God! That's incredible!" She wrapped her arms around him, offering a congratulatory embrace.

Owen had read a script several weeks earlier that had knocked his socks off. The role, a serious Denzel Washington-type part, would propel him out of sitcom land and into major motion picture superstardom. There were several huge names up for the role, but that hadn't stopped Owen from begging his manager to get him an audition. When they'd heard—through the Hollywood rumor mill—that auditions had already taken place, they'd figured he'd been knocked out of contention before even getting his shot.

"It's tomorrow."

"Oh. Shit. Wow. That's soon." Fiona tried to wrap her head around his bombshell.

"I know. The timing sucks. My manager just texted, said the casting director hadn't found anyone who felt like a good match."

"You have to go." She knew what this meant to Owen.

"Fee. How can I? We have the script to finish, and after last night…I feel like we need to…"

She shook her head. "Asher, Teddy and I can finish the script. It'll be easier without you there, encouraging us to succumb to happy hours and such."

He laughed at her joke but didn't bother to correct her. "Teddy's usually the bigger distraction."

"True."

"Which leads me to the next thing."

Fiona sighed. "There's more?"

"When I told Teddy about the audition, he insisted on flying back with me. There's a flight out of BWI in a few hours, and my manager has already sent the script to my place. Teddy said he'd run lines with me all night if necessary. Then I'll audition tomorrow night and fly back here the next day. We'd be gone less than forty-eight hours. I swear."

"Asher and I can make the tweaks. You go get that part. The rest can wait until you get back. We'll put everything else on hold."

Owen considered that, then shook his head, his expression serious. "No. Don't wait for me."

"What do you mean?" she asked.

"I think you and Asher should take the next couple of days to…" He appeared to struggle for the words. "I think the two of you should sleep together. Without me there. I mean…you and I have already done the deed. We know what things are like between us. Maybe you and Asher should take some time to see how you fit together. It might make it easier to put the pieces together when I get back."

Fiona liked that idea. More than she cared to admit. And she felt guilty as hell for it. They'd embarked on this thinking that they would be a threesome. Splitting up… Those words reminded her of something else he'd said, about knowing how things were between them.

"You know, I'll be honest with you, Owen. I don't even remember why we broke up the first time. I recall the fight, but not what it was about."

He chuckled. "It was Teddy's fault. Some friend of his in a fraternity wanted help killing half a keg leftover from a party the night before. Cardinal sin to return a keg with beer. I joined them for a couple drinks, which turned into a lot of drinks. Stood you up for a date. Woke up the next morning on the frat guy's couch. Teddy was passed out on the floor with his head in an empty pizza box, and I knew I was in trouble."

The light went on. "You avoided my calls all day, which pissed me off even more. And you were still hungover when you came by that night to apologize."

"Yeah. The headache didn't help. You yelled at me for being irresponsible and immature, and I lost my temper, started yelling back about you being clingy and needy and demanding. And—"

"And that was it."

"You wouldn't speak to me for nearly two weeks. Until Teddy intervened."

That part, Fiona remembered. "He tricked us. Invited me to go see *Silver Linings Playbook* with him."

"And I thought I was meeting him at the movies to see *Jack Reacher*."

Fiona laughed. She'd come face-to-face with Owen outside the theater and realized the anger wasn't there anymore. She had taken one look at him, with his guilt-ridden, apologetic smile, and forgiven the idiot in seconds. "Asshole had bought us all tickets to *Les Mis*, for God's sake."

"And that," Owen said, "was the end of 'Fiowen, the college years.'"

The friendship had resumed and Fiona hadn't looked back. Until Thursday night.

"Fee—" he started.

She shook her head. "Go catch your plane, Owen. And get that damn part. You were made for it. Made to be a star. Put the rest of this out of your mind until you get back."

He looked like he wanted to say more, but in the end, he simply sighed and stood.

Fiona rose as well and walked him to the door. "I'll see you in a couple of days. And in the meantime, I'm going back to bed. I'm worn out."

He put a finger under her chin and lifted her face to his, so she could see the humor in his eyes. Owen leaned closer and whispered in her ear, pretending to impart some big secret.

"You're crazy if you think you're going to get any sleep with Alpha Asher in your bed."

She laughed, realizing he'd meant what he said about her exploring things with Asher. One good look at his face proved he really wouldn't mind the two of them being together while he was gone. So she swatted at him, silently hoping his words were true because she wouldn't mind getting a little more worn out.

Owen turned before leaving, opening his arms, and she stepped into his embrace. "I love you so much. Have a good trip."

Owen placed a kiss on top of her head. “I love you too, Fee. See you soon.”

Chapter Ten

Asher stood in the hallway, listening as Owen and Fiona said their I love you's. When Owen hugged her goodbye, Asher's chest tightened. He wanted Fiona, wanted to be with her, but the sharing wasn't coming naturally. Hell, it wasn't coming at all.

Fiona turned around and spotted him. Her smile was wide and beautiful—and he knew in that moment there wasn't a damn thing in the world he wouldn't give her to make her happy.

"How long were you standing there?"

He shrugged. "Couple of minutes."

"Did you hear Owen got the audition?"

Asher's eyes widened. "You're kidding. The big one?"

She nodded, and explained Teddy and Owen would be gone for a couple of days, which left just the two of them to make the tweaks to the script. He didn't admit that he thought that might make the writing a hell of a lot easier. They'd been way too distracted since arriving in Baltimore. Maybe with just him and Fiona—

He realized the absurdity of that thought before he even had time to finish it. Being alone with her would be an even bigger distraction. And now, with Owen gone…

Asher would never be able to keep his hands off her.

"Owen should have stuck around a few minutes. I would have walked back to the hotel with him."

Fiona frowned. "You want to leave?"

Her question confused him and he shook his head. "Not at all." What he really wanted to do was take her back to her bedroom.

"Good." Fiona walked right up to him and wrapped her arms around his waist. He hadn't put his shirt back on when he woke up, too worried about the others when he found himself alone in the room.

"Good?" He cupped her cheeks in his hands, thrilled when she leaned closer, coming up on tiptoe to invite a kiss.

Asher gave in to her unspoken request. It wasn't hard. He held back nothing as he pushed her lips apart with his and touched his tongue to hers.

She pulled back quickly. "I should brush my teeth."

He didn't let go. "Not finished yet." He resumed the kiss, and this time Fiona offered no resistance, even going so far as to nip his lower lip.

He moaned. "Hungry?"

"Starving." One look in her eyes ensured she was thinking about the exact same thing he was, and it wasn't food.

"Owen—" he started.

"Isn't here and doesn't mind. Honest."

Asher wasn't sure that was entirely true, but he wasn't strong enough to put up an argument. He wanted her too badly. He tried to justify his actions when he grasped her hand and tugged her back to her bedroom by lamely reasoning Owen had made love to Fiona alone back when they were in college.

Maybe if Asher took this time, this chance to be with her alone, it would make it easier to accept Owen back into the bedroom later.

He locked the door behind them. Fiona turned and watched as he stalked toward her. She matched him step for step, moving backwards until she was next to the bed.

She sighed. "Twin mattress."

"We'll fit. I plan to spend the next few hours on top of you, not next to you."

Fiona reached down and untied the knot holding her robe in place. Then she shrugged it off. She was beautifully made, possessing an hourglass figure with trim legs—thanks to jogging—and the perfect amount of tits and ass.

"You're ogling."

One glance at her face proved she didn't mind at all.

"Appreciating," he corrected.

She looked toward his jeans and lifted her eyebrows suggestively.

He shook his head. "Always in a hurry."

Asher pushed her until her knees hit the bed. She sat down on the mattress and started to crawl into place, but he stopped her, kneeling in front of her with a firm grip on her legs.

Parting them, he leaned forward, running his tongue along her slit from anus to clit.

"Fuck," Fiona breathed out. "How did you hide the fact you were a sex maniac all these years?"

He chuckled. "We weren't exactly hanging out in the bedroom together."

"So much wasted time. So many mistakes."

"I don't know if I'd call the Brock and Christina years mistakes. I figure if we learned something from them, it's better to think of it as experience."

Before she could reply, he pressed his tongue to her clit then sucked on it. Fiona fell backwards, holding herself up with her elbows on the bed so she could watch him. He took advantage of the change in position, lifting her legs over his shoulders to hold her open. Asher was a big fan of foreplay, had spent years mastering the art form.

Fiona clearly appreciated his efforts, throwing her head back, crying out each time he touched her clit the right way. When he thrust his tongue inside her, she fell all the way back, nearly hitting her head on the wall.

"I can't take it. Too good. Need you. Inside me."

He lifted his head, grinning. "You realize we're just getting started."

"That's not funny," she groaned.

"That's not a joke. Jesus, woman. Have you ever had sex that lasted more than twenty minutes?"

The fact that she paused to consider the answer to that question drove him insane.

"Brock was a bigger loser than I thought."

"He wasn't a—"

Asher pushed two fingers in her pussy, cutting off any protest she might have made on Brock's behalf. It was time the two of them left their lovers in the past. He was going to stop thinking about Christina, and he was going to make damn sure she couldn't remember Brock's name by the end of the day.

Owen… Well, Owen was another thing.

Asher pushed that concern away too. He'd waited too fucking long to get Fiona in his arms. He wasn't going to be anywhere other than here and now.

Fiona matched the rhythm of his thrusting fingers, her inner muscles clenching tightly. As always, she was racing toward the finish line.

She cursed when he pulled his fingers out.

"Where's your vibrator?"

"What?"

"I know you packed it. Where is it?"

"Suitcase under the bed."

Asher reached under the bed, pulling out her bag. Flipping the lid open, he grinned when he found not just the mother of all vibrators, but a tube of lubrication on top of everything else in the case. She hadn't lied about her toy. It was pretty impressive.

He waved the monster at her. "You couldn't find a bigger one?"

"Intimidated?" she teased.

"I'll let you decide that for yourself later."

Fiona pushed back up on her elbows, her legs still parted with him tucked between. She looked at the vibrator with a worried expression.

"What's wrong?" he asked.

"We're going to have sex, right? I mean…I *really* want to. Want to be with you."

He understood her concern. "We're having sex. Lots of it. All day. The vibrator is for your second and third orgasms."

"What happened to number one?"

"That one's going to be on my fingers."

"And the fourth?"

"And fifth will be with me buried deep inside you."

She gave him a sassy grin. "Five orgasms? Big talker."

"Big doer." He placed the vibrator and lube on the mattress and bent his head back down. He'd promised to take his time and he meant it. For the better part of fifteen minutes, he sucked, nipped and played, as Fiona begged and cursed for repletion. She found it fast when Asher filled her with three fingers. He thrust less than a dozen times, then had to reach up to cover her mouth with his hand when she came loudly. He didn't have a clue if any of her cousins were in the apartment, but there was no way they didn't know what was going on inside this room.

With any luck, the male Collins cousins had cleared out.

Fiona lay sideways on the bed, a thin sheen of sweat on her brow. She was breathing heavily, her eyelids heavy as her gaze rested on him.

"That was only number one?" she asked.

He nodded.

"I don't think I can take another one of those."

"Another four," Asher said with a laugh as he stood and turned her so that she lay on the bed properly, her head on the pillow. Then he tucked himself next to her. It was a tight squeeze, but with her nestled in his arms, they fit.

For a couple of minutes, she lay quietly in his embrace, and he thought maybe she'd fallen asleep. Then she lifted her head, and it was the most natural thing in the world to bend his and kiss her.

Their lips took and gave and explored. He kissed her cheeks, the side of her neck and teased her earlobes with his teeth. Then Fiona did the same, raining kisses on his jaw and down along his chest.

The exhaustion that had been rife on her face a few minutes earlier had vanished. When her hand drifted along the front of his jeans, he knew she was ready for round two.

"Not so fast," he said, gripping her wrist. "There's still the issue of orgasm number two."

"And three. Yeah, yeah. I want to see you." Fiona tried to tug her hand away, intent on touching him.

Asher wasn't sure why he was resistant to exposing himself to her.

It was probably that stupid joke getting into his head, Owen and Teddy constantly ribbing him, calling him Biggus Dickus, the name ripped straight from a *Monty Python* movie.

The problem was, they weren't really exaggerating, and he'd dated more than a couple girls in high school who'd taken one look and said "no thanks."

Of course, on the flipside, he was pretty sure his cock was what had gotten his foot in the door with Christina.

"Ash—" she started.

He cut her off, sitting up to retrieve the vibrator from the foot of her bed. The size of it gave him some peace of mind. He studied the toy, making note of all the bells and whistles. "Cadillac of vibrators," he murmured, recalling her joke at the pub Thursday night.

She giggled softly and he heard the nervousness in the sound.

"You have used this, right?"

She nodded. "Yeah. I got it a few weeks ago. Wanted to see…"

Asher wasn't misreading. Something was bothering her. "Wanted to see what?"

Fiona lifted one shoulder. "See how…I did…with…"

He laughed as the light went on. "You bought this because of *me*? Because of that joke?"

She flushed bright red. "Don't flatter yourself."

"Don't lie. The guys keep joking about the Biggus Dickus thing and you wanted to see if you could handle it."

She waved her hand, pshawing like he'd said something utterly ridiculous.

He let her off the hook and stopped teasing her. He knew the truth even if she didn't want to admit it. There was something he needed to know more. "What do you think of it?"

Fiona reached out and touched the toy longingly. "I love it. The way it fills me up. At first, I thought it'll never fit, then something loosened and, God…"

Asher didn't have to hear anything more. He moved between her legs and ran his fingers along her slit. She was still wet, so ready. He placed the tip of the vibrator at her opening and slowly pressed it in.

There was a bit of resistance as her muscles sought to accept the large toy, but then, it was just as she said. Something gave way and it slid in easily. He stopped with a couple of inches of the shaft to go and turned it on.

Fiona's hands flew to his shoulders and he bent over her, thrusting the vibrator in and out as she clung to him.

He kept the speed slow and steady at first, letting the vibrations of the toy do their thing. But Fiona wasn't satisfied with easy.

"Faster. Please!"

He complied, setting her off like a bottle rocket. The second orgasm came quicker than he expected. He'd told Owen to pay attention, to read the signs, but Asher had been too entranced by her cries, too turned on by the way her fingers gripped his shoulders, holding him as if he was the only thing that mattered.

He pulled the toy out when her orgasm waned and tossed it aside, caging her beneath him, kissing her even as she struggled to catch her breath.

"Need. You," she gasped.

Asher rose from the bed and unfastened his jeans, tugging them down along with his boxers.

Fiona sat up as his erection was revealed, her eyes widening.

He let her look her fill, forcing himself to give her time to decide. Asher was thrust back to high school when his first love, Paige, had taken one look at him and said, "That's not natural."

How many times in his life had those words drifted through his mind? He shut them down and braced himself.

Fiona didn't say anything.

Instead, she wrapped her palm around his dick, kissing then licking along the shaft.

No woman had *ever* attempted a blowjob. Not even Christina.

Yet Fiona opened her mouth and took the head of his cock inside, sucking on it as if it were made of ice cream.

His hands flew to the side of her head, gripping her hair. "Fee—"

She released him with a soft pop. "I need you inside me. Right now."

Asher pushed her to her back, climbing over her. Her legs were open, inviting. He reached for the lubrication, but she shook her head. "Don't need it."

"Princess," he murmured. "I don't want to hurt you."

"You won't."

He glanced toward the floor, cursing himself for forgetting to grab the condom.

Once again, Fiona stopped him.

"On birth control. Please, Ash! You're killing me."

He'd heard those words more than a few times when he was inside a lover, but not when he was still on the outside.

But in the end, he stopped fighting his doubts. This was Fiona, his best friend, who was honest to a fault.

She wouldn't lie, not even to protect his feelings, so he had to believe her when she said she wanted him.

Thank God.

He pressed the head inside, moving slowly, watching and waiting for the moment when it became too much.

Like with the vibrator, he felt that brief moment of resistance and then…ease.

He pushed in halfway, then stopped, withdrawing a little before returning. She was wet and hot and felt *so* damn good.

Fiona pressed up against him on each downward thrust, and he fought to keep control.

"Dammit, Asher. Fuck me like you mean it! Stop being a freaking Boy Scout. I won't break."

He dropped to his elbows and gave in—to her demands and his desires.

Asher deepened his thrusts, and when she didn't complain—he was fairly certain "fuck me harder" wasn't a complaint—he moved faster…and yes, harder.

Fiona wrapped her legs around his waist and tilted her hips, and before he could slow his return thrust, he was all the way inside her.

He froze, partly out of concern for her and because it felt so fucking good.

Fiona dug her fingers into his shoulders, the nails piercing slightly.

"Fee."

"You stopped again."

It took him a second to wrap his head around her comment. She thought he was toying with her, attempting to draw out the anticipation.

Jesus.

He was a split second away from coming, and he wouldn't have to move to do it.

"I'm never letting you go, Fiona. Ever."

It was a pretty heavy sentiment to lay on her, considering where they were and what they were doing, but he wouldn't take it back. He'd never meant anything more.

She gave him a sweet smile. "Ash?"

"Yeah?"

"I swear to God if you don't finish this right now, I'll cut that monster cock of yours off. Pop Pop has to have hedge clippers around here somewhere."

He laughed, even as he started to move, tried to wrap his head around the fact he was really inside her. Fiona. His Fee. His fantasies over the years didn't hold a candle to the reality. What's more, he wasn't wearing a condom. Another first for him. There was something primal and maybe even a little caveman about it, but he liked the idea of coming inside her.

Fiona really had been close. Three more thrusts and she was coming.

On the fourth, he fell with her.

Asher held himself above her for a few minutes, then slowly, gingerly withdrew.

She curled against his chest when he hit his back.

"Did I hurt you?"

"What?" Asher asked, thinking that was usually his question.

"My nails. I think I scratched you."

"I'm fine, Fee."

They lay there together in the silence, reveling in what had just happened. Asher tried not to acknowledge the very large part of him that was glad Owen wasn't there. What happened this morning felt right, perfect, while last night had been…off.

He'd think about that later. Now wasn't the time. Especially when Fiona said, "I don't mean to nitpick, but I was promised five orgasms. That was only three."

It was all he needed to hear. He spent the rest of the day giving her not only numbers four and five, but six and seven as well.

Chapter Eleven

After spending the better part of Sunday in Fiona's bed, she and Asher had declared Monday all business. Or at least, mostly business.

Okay, half real business, half monkey business.

Fiona rolled over in the king-size bed they'd stolen from Teddy in the suite and grinned as Asher slept the sleep of the dead, passed out on his stomach, his face turned toward hers, resting on the pillow as he breathed deeply, steadily.

They'd set up a reward system. For each scene they successfully revised and reworked, they granted themselves thirty minutes of fooling around, but not sex. That was the big carrot, the grand prize that Asher called "completion for completion."

After ten hours of work, interspersed with kissing, fondling, sucking and stroking, they'd both been panting by the time they'd finally finished the fucking script.

Her stomach growled. She'd eaten precious little in the past two days, sating her hunger in other ways.

But now, her body ached in all the right places, and her stomach was done waiting for its turn. She walked out to the living room and grabbed her cell.

"Hey, Yvonne," she said when her cousin answered the phone. "Any chance I could get a couple of tonight's specials bagged up to go?"

Yvonne put the orders in for her, and they chatted a couple minutes more about the script…and then, her cousin less than subtly inquired whether or not Fiona would be sleeping in her own bed tonight.

She said no, ignored Yvonne's "I knew it!" and hung up, promising to be there in half an hour to get the food.

"Fee?" Asher called out from the bedroom.

"Out here."

He was in the doorway before she made it two steps back toward the bedroom. Like her, he hadn't bothered to tug on any clothes. They'd actually spent the last two hours writing in nothing but their underwear.

"Come back to bed," he said in that deep, grumbly voice that had her body responding before her mind could engage.

She started to walk toward him, then her stomach growled again. She stopped. "No. Food. I'm going to throw my clothes back on and head over to the pub. I placed a couple of take-out orders for us. Plus, I want to grab my toothbrush and pajamas."

"Forget about the pajamas. You won't need them. Bring the vibrator instead. I want to use it on you again."

She shivered at the thought, recalling how incredible it had felt when he'd used the toy on her. So much better than when she played with it herself.

Asher grinned as her face grew hot with the thought. "Come on. Let's get dressed and get the food. Otherwise, we'll never get there."

The two of them threw on their clothes and held hands as they walked along the cobblestone streets of

Fell's Point. Out in the fresh air, the thick, heavy desire that seemed impenetrable in the hotel eased, and she was able to walk and talk without the thought of sex constantly buzzing in her ears.

Sex with Asher was highly addictive.

She was surprised when he bypassed the pub and led her toward the waterfront instead, but she didn't hesitate to follow him. It was a beautiful spring night and like him, she was happy to be outside in it.

Once they reached the water, he found a bench for them to sit on. They watched the lights from the boats and surrounding buildings twinkle on the smooth, glassy surface of the water.

"Fiona, these past two days have been some of the best of my life."

She smiled. "Mine too. Can I ask you something?"

"Of course."

"The sex thing." She tried to figure out how to phrase her questions. Asher really did seem like a different man in the bedroom, so domineering, so alpha. She wasn't so innocent to believe that they probably hadn't scratched the surface of his experience. "It's pretty intense and…"

"Out of character?"

She shook her head. "No…yes…maybe? Where did that guy come from?"

He sighed. "You really want to talk about Christina?"

"No. Not exactly. I mean, I figured a lot of this…" She waved her hand around, her vocabulary failing her.

"This?" he questioned, but she didn't answer. She could feel her face growing hot despite the cool breeze, which basically answered his question for him.

"The dominance? The hair pulling? The bondage?"

She nodded. "There's more, isn't there?"

Asher rested his arm along the back of the bench and she shifted closer, loving how it felt to nestle into him. "Yeah. There's more. But, Fiona, I would never do anything without talking to you first, without making sure it was something you wanted too."

"I know that." She did. Because despite the beast who emerged in the bedroom, at heart, Asher was her Boy Scout, and that seemed to be the stronger trait.

"I like what we've done. A lot. More than I know how to say."

"I love being with you, Fiona."

"I'm just wondering if…we could…"

She stopped. It was on the tip of her tongue to ask if they could drop ménage from the kink list. God, she wanted to do everything else, but *that*…that wasn't working for her.

However, Asher had been the one to instigate the threesome and, despite her reservations about it, she didn't want to disappoint him if it was something he wanted.

Something he needed.

"We're going to explore it all, Fee. There's so much I—we—want to do with you." He paused before leaning closer to whisper, "To you."

She shivered, and the hormones she'd managed to shake off on the walk reemerged full force, and she reconsidered her request. They'd only tried it once. Maybe she wasn't giving the idea a fair shake. After all, she'd loved everything else.

Owen would return tomorrow. Which gave her one more night alone with her sexy, commanding lover. She'd take advantage of it. Then tomorrow, she'd simply have to trust that Asher knew how to guide her and Owen the rest of the way.

"Let's hurry up and get the food," she said, standing and heading back toward the pub.

***

Asher didn't chastise her for, once again, trying to rush to the good stuff. He took her hand and they walked back together. Yvonne had their food ready for them, so Asher said he'd wait at the bar while Fiona ran upstairs to pack an overnight bag.

Tris was behind the counter while Patrick was in what Fiona called his usual spot, dead center of the long, shiny mahogany bar.

"Pull up a seat, son," Patrick offered.

Asher placed the food on the counter and refused Tris's offer of a drink. He was in too much of a hurry to get Fiona back to the hotel. The clock was ticking on their time alone. They only had one more night together before Owen returned, and Asher intended to make it count.

"Yvonne reports that the two of you finished your script," Patrick said.

Asher suspected there was very little her Pop Pop didn't know about what was happening in his children's and grandchildren's lives—big stuff and small.

"Yep. It's in the can. Rest of the cast will arrive on Thursday."

"I hope my line didn't change," Patrick mused. "I think I've finally figured out a great way to say it to make it funny."

Asher chuckled at the older man's enthusiasm over appearing in the sitcom. The plan was to film the show right after the bar closed one night the next week. They'd tried to figure out a way to avoid closing the pub down for real business. Since the show's script took place at night, and because they wanted to limit the number of people who saw it before it aired, they'd opted to film it at two a.m. on Monday night. They'd scheduled practices at that same late hour for Friday and Saturday nights, with a dress rehearsal Sunday at midnight—since the pub closed earlier that day. Apart from the cast and a handful of hired extras, everyone else on the set would be Fiona's family. Tris and Padraig would be behind the bar, Yvonne and Sunnie waiting tables, and the rest of her aunts, uncles and cousins were lined up to be patrons.

"We didn't touch that line," Asher reassured Patrick. "It was perfect from the start."

"Looking forward to Teddy getting back. I didn't get to talk to him much. Everyone keeps telling me he's a funny guy, but all I got was the boring polite routine reserved for ancient grandfathers."

Asher laughed. "Give him a couple shots of whiskey and he'll forget to be on his best behavior."

"So noted. Fiona said Owen got called back to Hollywood for a big audition."

Asher nodded, his chest going tight at the mention of Owen's name. Then he realized something in his face had caught Patrick's attention.

"Will that work for the show or does this mean the sitcom will end?"

"Oh, no. Filming for the movie would happen when *Wild Winters* is on hiatus. We've got a contract with the studio for two more seasons."

"That's good. So if it's not the audition bothering you, what is?"

Asher wasn't sure how to reply.

"I'm an old man, Asher. I don't have time to beat around the bush. I mention Teddy, you laugh. I say Owen's name, you frown. So, I'll ask again. What's the problem with him?"

Asher wasn't sure confiding in Fiona's granddaddy was the smartest thing to do, but he'd had too many worries bottled up since Saturday night.

"He's, um…Owen is…"

"Interested in my granddaughter?"

"Wow. You aren't kidding about just laying it out there, are you?" Asher raised his hand toward Tris. "I changed my mind. I'll have a Jack and Coke."

Tris shot his father a look, but Patrick raised his hands, palms up. "What?"

"You driving Asher to drink?"

"We're talking. There's nothing wrong with talking," Patrick insisted.

Tris put Asher's drink down in front of him and shot his Pop an "I'm watching you" look before walking away.

"Owen has been in love with Fiona since college."

"He told you this?"

Asher nodded, recalling that night senior year, how drunk and depressed Owen had been over losing her. "Yeah. He did."

"So," Patrick said, "what do you intend to do about it?"

"Do?" Asher asked, swallowing heavily. "About what?"

"Don't play stupid, son. You're *not* stupid. You know what I'm talking about."

Asher choked on the sip of drink he'd just taken, and Tris, who'd walked to the end of the bar, glanced their way, scowling. When Patrick rolled his eyes, Tris continued to take another patron's order.

Patrick turned his attention back to him with a chuckle. "Take it easy, my boy. If you can't say it yet, I'll say it for you. You're in love with my granddaughter."

Asher felt as if he was standing on shaky ground. The Collins men were known for being overprotective of the women in their family. How the hell was he supposed to reply to Patrick's accurate assessment?

And what the hell did the older man expect him to do about his feelings?

"Have you told Fiona how you feel?" Patrick asked.

"Sort of."

Patrick frowned. "How do you *sort of* tell a woman you love her?"

"I proposed a ménage."

Asher held his breath, waiting for the man to either laugh him out of the pub, or call Tris back over to kick his ass.

Patrick did neither. "A noble suggestion. That won't work in your case."

"Why not? It worked for Sean and Killian."

"Different situations entirely. Both of them were okay with sharing the loves of their lives with their best friends. I don't think you are."

Asher ran his finger along his glass, wiping at the condensation left there by the ice. Patrick was right.

"I hate it. Every time Owen touches her, kisses her…I want to punch him in the face."

"I'm sure you do."

"The thing is, me, Owen, Fee and Teddy have been friends for a long time. We're practically family. No. We *are* family. And in Owen's case, we're his *only* family. I can't do anything to screw that up."

"Have you asked Fiona how *she* feels?" Tris asked.

Asher glanced up, surprised to see Fiona's uncle standing there. It was clear he'd been eavesdropping the entire time.

Patrick chuckled. "And you call *me* nosy."

Asher answered Tris's question, grateful to have people to talk to about this. "I suggested the threesome idea and she went for it."

"Happily? Or is she pretending like you are, afraid of hurting you and Owen?"

Asher didn't know how to respond—because he hadn't asked her outright. She'd said she was okay with it during the Truth or Dare game, but then she'd lost her nerve when their shirts came off. Asher had been too preoccupied with his own uneasiness due to Owen's presence that he hadn't really taken the time to see if she felt the same.

Since then, they'd been on their own, without Owen.

And it had been perfect.

Bliss.

Patrick gave him an understanding smile as he said the words Asher didn't want to hear. "You're going to have to buck up, son, and tell Fiona and Owen the truth."

"What if she wants all or nothing? Or what if…" Asher forced himself to voice his biggest fear. "What if she chooses him?"

Tris leaned forward, resting his arms on the counter. "I've lived a lot of my life thinking there was happiness in playing it safe, waiting for the right time. Then I met Lane, my wife, and I realized sometimes the only thing you can do is jump into the flames. This last year reminded me of that again as I watched my son with Mia…saw him open his heart to her even knowing how it would end. There's a lot to be said for just opening your heart and going for it because even feeling the way he does now, Padraig has said more than once he'd do it all again in a heartbeat. And I know that's the truth."

Patrick placed a firm hand on his shoulder and squeezed. "Life's too short, Asher," he said softly.

"I'm ready," Fiona said, stepping up behind them. "Hey, Pop Pop." She gave her grandfather a kiss on the cheek. "Been keeping Asher entertained?" She caught sight of Asher's drink and lifted it, taking a sip. "With bourbon?"

They all chuckled.

"Did you want to hang out for a while?" she asked.

Asher shook his head, Tris and Patrick's words striking deep and true. He and Fiona needed to talk. "No. We better head back or our food will get cold."

He reached for his wallet, but Tris waved his money away. "I'll put it on Owen's tab."

"Thanks," Asher said, looking at Tris, and then Patrick. "For everything."

He grabbed the bag and Fiona's hand.

She waited until they hit the street to ask the question he knew was coming. "Thanks?"

Asher rolled his eyes. Of course she'd picked up on that. "Your Pop Pop and uncle were giving me some advice."

"Advice about?"

"You."

"Oh, shit. Listen. You already know all my faults, Ash. I'm opinionated and stubborn. I tend to think I know best on pretty much everything, and I might have a teeny-tiny princess complex."

"Three tiaras in your desk drawer at work and the fact that you packed one—"

"Two," she interjected.

"Two," he continued, "for your trip to Baltimore, does not constitute 'teeny-tiny.'"

She smirked. "I regret nothing. Apologize for nothing."

He wrapped his arm around her shoulders. "Do you really think your Pop Pop and Tris would try to scare me away from you?"

She shrugged, then admitted, "Not unless they didn't like you."

"Have they ever done that?"

Fiona nodded. "Last Christmas. With Brock. And only because the manly-man intimidation tactics hadn't worked the few times Mr. Big Gesture had come home with me before that. I think they were getting desperate and decided to take a different approach. Guess I should have seen the writing on the wall about Brock then."

They had just reached the hotel and Fiona stopped walking. "So, if they weren't warning you away, what was the advice about?"

Before Asher could reply, they heard someone calling Fiona's name.

"Fee! Fiona!"

Fiona glanced back toward the direction they'd just come, her eyes widening. "Mom? Dad?"

"Tris said we might catch you if we hurried," Teagan said breathlessly.

Fiona turned away from Asher, her question forgotten when her parents jogged up to them. She was clearly equal parts surprised and delighted.

"There's my girl," Sky said, giving her a big bear hug. "I swear you look more like your mom every day. Beautiful."

Fiona rolled her eyes, making it clear her father made that comparison often, then she recalled Asher was there.

Asher had spent quite a bit of time with Sky and Teagan in the past, going out to dinners or chilling with them at Fiona's place whenever they came for visits.

Her mom hugged him after releasing her daughter, and Sky shook his hand.

"You were just here for Mia's memorial. I thought you had a show in New York," Fiona said.

"We did it. But I didn't get enough time with either of you girls last week."

Asher recalled Fiona saying her parents were in the midst of a mini-tour, so they had only been able to stop in for the day of the memorial, taking off that night for a big show at Madison Square Garden.

"Besides," Teagan added, "there was no way we were missing everyone's big TV debut at the pub."

Fiona looked uncomfortable and a little bit panicked. "You know you two can't be in the show, right? You're too big, too recognizable. We didn't write parts for you. If Sky Mitchell and Teagan Collins show up on *Wild Winters*, we'd have to rewrite the whole thing."

Teagan rolled her eyes. "We're not here to crash your show, sweetheart. We were hoping we could watch with you during the filming. Al let us do that the last time we were in California. I didn't want to wait until the show came out to see Pop deliver his big line. Every single time we talk on the phone these days, he runs through it for me a few times."

Sky groaned. "Then he makes her hand the phone to me so *I* can analyze it. I'm a singer, not an actor."

They all laughed. "We've both heard him say it a few thousand times too," Fiona added. "To pretty much every patron at the bar. It's a good thing it's not a major plot spoiler, or he would have given the whole premise of the show away."

"Are you guys still working tonight?" Teagan asked.

Asher shook his head. "No." He lifted the takeout. "Late dinner. We're finished with the script tweaks. Nothing more to do until the cast arrives and read-throughs and rehearsals begin. We just hang around the set, in case anything falls flat and we need to rework lines."

"So you're free?" Teagan asked Fiona. "I was hoping I could convince you to spend the night with us on the bus tonight for a laugh."

Sky grinned widely. "Your mother is going through some sort of delayed empty-nest thing. All she could talk about on the way into Maryland was how much she misses all the times you girls used to curl up on the big bed in our room and watch romantic comedies as we barreled down the highway.

"I pulled out a few for tonight," Teagan said. "Thought we could do a Meg Ryan-a-thon. *You've Got Mail, When Harry Met Sally* and *Sleepless in Seattle*."

Fiona glanced back at Asher, obviously torn since the two of them had made plans for dinner—and then after-dinner plans that included burning off what they'd just eaten.

He let her off the hook easy. He knew how much Fiona missed her parents. Their visits were always highly anticipated as they were too few and far between.

"Go spend the night with your parents. It sounds like a lot of fun." He gestured to the food. "Leaves more for me."

Fiona wasn't as easily convinced. "Maybe you could hang out with us a little while."

Asher shook his head. "Nope. It's obviously girls' night. I'll see you tomorrow." Because he didn't know how much her parents knew about the two of them, he gave her a quick, friendly kiss on the cheek, then waved, saying goodbye before Fiona could continue to protest.

As he walked to the elevator, he decided he was actually glad her parents had shown up. Life had been a whirlwind since his arrival in Baltimore, and he thought it might be nice to have a few quiet hours to reflect on what was happening.

Tris and Patrick had given him a lot to think about.

Then his cell phone rang. A glance at the screen showed it was Owen.

"Hey, Owen," Asher said when he picked up the phone, walking into the suite at the same time. "How was the audition?"

"It was amazing." For several minutes, Owen filled him in on all the details and how good he felt about it. Asher was thrilled for his friend, but he found his thoughts constantly drifting back to Saturday night in Fiona's bedroom.

He considered bringing it up, but this wasn't a conversation for a phone call. If it went south, Owen was on the opposite coast and too far away for Asher to fix it.

"About the other night—" Owen started.

Asher sighed. "Listen, Owen—"

"No. Let me say this. I love you and Fee, you know that, right?"

"Of course."

"You guys and Teddy are my family. I feel bad about what I said at karaoke."

Asher didn't reply. Apparently, he'd been thinking about the wrong night. "What did you say?"

"That comment about no one ever looking at me like Fiona's family looks at her. *You* guys do. I shouldn't have sounded like such a whiny dick. You don't have to share blood to be family. The way you and Fee finished the script so I could do this audition, the way Teddy came back with me to run lines and keep me calm…I'm the luckiest bastard on the planet, and I know it. I'm sorry for what I said."

Asher had never received a more unnecessary apology. Or one that made him feel worse about what he planned to say the next time he and Owen were together.

"Owen. You don't need to apologize for that. I feel the same way. You're the brother I never had. And Fee and Teddy are the sisters—"

He let Owen's loud laughter drown out the rest of the joke.

"Cool." With his peace spoken, Owen bounced right back to the audition, chatting another ten minutes about every single thing the casting director had said to him, the studio's plans for the movie and twenty-seven-thousand other things. He hadn't heard if he got the part yet, but that didn't seem to matter to him. There was no denying Owen's feet weren't touching the ground.

When they hung up, Asher glanced at the bag of take-out food, but he'd lost his appetite.

He'd made a mistake of epic proportions, convincing himself a threesome was the answer and then plowing headfirst into it, without thinking about what would happen if it went south.

It was then that Asher was forced to admit something to himself. He was a cocky bastard at heart, who didn't fail often. Typically, he could put his mind to something and make it work, no matter what.

This didn't fall into that category, and to make it worse, he wasn't just hurting himself. He was taking Owen and Fiona down as well. Things were amazing when it was just him and Fiona, but more than a few times, he'd wondered if she was wishing Owen was with them. After her initial nervousness wore off last weekend, she'd been all-in, and Asher suspected she'd regretted it when he'd taken sex off the table.

As for Owen…the guy just said they were his family. After so many years of being passed from one relative to the next, Owen had never felt wanted. How the fuck could Asher make him feel the same way?

He couldn't.

He walked toward the bedroom, stripped off his clothes and lay down, as one word kept drifting through his brain on auto-repeat.

Shit.

Chapter Twelve

Tuesday arrived, but Owen didn't. Instead, he'd texted to say he and Teddy had read and loved their revisions to the script. As such, they'd decided to fly back to Baltimore with the rest of the cast on the studio's private plane on Thursday so they could run lines on the flight.

Fiona felt guilty about her happiness in stealing two more nights alone with Asher, wondering for the hundredth time how to broach the subject of Owen and Asher's threesome dream. In the end, she kept her concerns to herself and took full advantage of the extra alone time.

Tuesday night started with a bubble bath and ended with her tied to the hotel bed, spread-eagle, while Asher did dirty, naughty, amazing things to her. Wednesday's sexual escapades included a spanking and her vibrator—and Asher, damn him, was actually making her a believer when it came to anal play. Even Happy Clam was starting to be convinced.

According to Asher, the audition had gone very well, so when Owen showed up at the pub with Teddy and the cast on Thursday night, his spirits were still sky-high, and everyone was more than ready to help him celebrate.

Fiona watched the first round of drinks go down, and then the second. Asher pulled her aside.

"He's happy."

Fiona was thinking the same thing. "Really happy. Happier than I think I've seen him in a long time."

"Yeah. I know. I was sitting here trying to figure out the last time I saw him like this."

"That's easy," Fiona said. "It was the day we found out the network was optioning *Wild Winters*."

"Oh yeah. Owen didn't land for a week. It was great," Asher said, smiling as he recalled Owen's utter ecstasy. "It's funny. Seeing him now makes me think that lately…"

Asher didn't finish his statement, but his words matched her very thoughts at the moment. "That he hasn't been himself the past year or so. I hadn't noticed it until tonight. Didn't realize he was unhappy until I saw him *really* happy."

"Yeah."

It was obvious neither of them was sure what to do with that information. Fiona tucked it away, promising to bring it up to Owen when they were all back in California.

Then she considered the other conversation that had to happen first—and she sent up a silent prayer that Owen would still be speaking to her once they returned to the West Coast.

"I think I'm going to spend the night upstairs," Fiona said, wishing she'd figured out a better reason for doing so than the lame excuse she was about to offer. It had taken her nearly an hour to come up with the stupid "we need our sleep and none of us will get it if I go back with you guys tonight" line.

To her surprise, Asher didn't ask for an excuse. "That's probably a good idea. The next few days are going to get nuts around here with rehearsals and filming. Add in the cast and crew and the Collinses, and it's going to be tough to steal some time just for us."

Fiona considered Asher's use of "us," knowing that most likely included Owen. She needed to talk to them—together—to explain her feelings, but Asher had a great point. They were facing long days surrounded by way too many people, who would all be placing demands on them.

Not to mention…Owen's happiness.

Or Asher's, for that matter. Sleeping in his arms had been bliss for her, but had Asher wished Owen was there with them? The more she was with Asher, the more evident it became that his sexual prowess was off the charts. Maybe threesome sex, like bondage, was part of his sexual makeup. Something he wanted…needed, even.

Fiona was in no hurry to potentially hurt either—or both—of her best friends, but she also wasn't the type to sit around and hold her tongue. If only the timing on all of this wasn't so shitty.

"So, we party like it's 1999?" Fiona asked, as Prince's hit started playing.

"Hell yeah." Asher grabbed her hand, leading her to the dance floor, where they were joined by Teddy and Owen. The four of them danced with reckless abandon, a pack of lunatics, laughing and shouting the lyrics and living for the moment.

These were the times that Fiona loved best.

Just the four of them.

Young. Free. Wild.

Their joke about waiting for Owen to land held a grain of truth, because he didn't. The man was a thousand feet high and untouchable. According to

Asher, by the time they returned to the hotel that night—sans her—Owen and Teddy took the room with two queen beds, giving Asher the king room. Apart from giving her a hello hug and quick kiss on the cheek when he got in, Owen hadn't really touched her. More than that, she got a sense he was avoiding her. He was acting like their night together had never happened. Business as usual.

Friday had been a weird day. They had all agreed to sleep in until two in the afternoon in order to "switch their internal clocks" so they were ready for the two a.m. practices starting that night.

Fiona wished she'd managed it. Sleep had eluded her, so instead, she and her parents met for breakfast, then she wound up waiting around for hours, fretting over her love life. It had gone from nonexistent to seriously complicated in the blink of an eye. She had considered talking to her mom about it, but in the end, she held her tongue, simply telling her mom about the breakup with Brock.

By the time the guys woke up that day, Al and the rest of the cast were in the hotel suite, running lines, and Fiona was swept up in the general hubbub. She hadn't managed to buy any time alone with Asher or Owen. Worse than that was the fact neither of them appeared to even want to sneak away to talk about things between them.

The same thing avoidance mingled with nonstop activity surrounding the show had happened Saturday, and then they'd spent nearly fourteen hours on Sunday bouncing around the city, doing location shots. She was grateful for the reprieve even as she constantly wondered what the hell was going on.

She'd decided enough was enough. She would wait until they filmed the finale and then she was putting her foot down, grabbing both Owen and Asher and making them sit down and talk to her.

Fiona had spent three days praying for Monday, and now that it had arrived, she was bundle of nerves and nothing was any better. Earlier today, during a meeting with the cast and crew, Owen had asked her, Asher and Teddy to stand next to him and had called them his family, his best friends, and the best things that ever happened to him. He claimed *Wild Winters* wouldn't exist without them. Everyone had lifted a glass and toasted the team, and while Fiona was touched by his comments, her gut had churned with all the things they had yet to say.

How would he feel about her after she told him she was in love with Asher?

Just Asher?

And what if Asher wanted all or nothing? What if she wasn't enough? There was no question she was far more inexperienced sexually than he was. What if he craved someone with more knowledge? Someone like Christina?

The night of filming had finally arrived and instead of being excited, Fiona was annoyed and frustrated. And okay, horny. Happy Clam was no longer satisfied hitching a ride with the Cadillac of vibrators. She wanted Asher.

She hovered by the doorway to the apartment, watching the beehive of activity, unaware she was frowning until Sunnie approached her.

"Holy crap. What is going on with you, Fiona? You went from laid and happy to," Sunnie ran her finger up and down with a grimace, "whatever this grumpy-Gus thing is."

Fiona looked at Sunnie with a scowl. "Owen and Asher are avoiding me."

"Why?"

She shrugged. "I don't know why. We went from getting it on last weekend to this weekend, where neither one of them will touch me. No kisses, no hand-holding. I'm starting to think I misread everything. I thought they wanted a threesome, but now I'm afraid they don't want anything at all. What if they're trying to figure out how to break things off?"

That uncomfortable thought hadn't hit her until this morning when she woke up alone. Again.

For the past couple of days, she'd been trying to figure out how to tell Asher she didn't want a threesome and Owen that she didn't…want *him*. God. She couldn't even think about saying those words without her stomach doing a million flip-flops.

Now the idea that they might be stressing about letting her down easy was killing her.

Sunnie shook her head. "They'd be fools to do that. You're the bomb, the best. I bet they're both just worked up over the finale. Tomorrow, everything will fall into place."

"Thanks, Sunnie. I hope that's true."

Her cousin drifted over to where a large group of their family stood, excitedly talking, all of them thrilled by the chance to be extras. Padraig had returned home that morning, and she was relieved to see that he looked better. The dark circles under his eyes were gone, and he seemed much more like the old Paddy as he smiled and chatted with the others. There was no way he'd ever get over Mia, but it looked like he was maybe starting to find a way to move on.

Fiona didn't join them. She'd be a buzzkill. While she appreciated Sunnie's support, she'd had too many sleepless nights since Thursday. She was a woman at the end of her rope. It ended tonight.

As soon as filming wrapped, she was pulling her elusive men away from the crowd and they were talking it out. All of it.

Unfortunately…that wasn't happening right now.

While the pub had closed a couple hours earlier, the place was buzzing as spotlights and cameras were set up, positioned and then repositioned. Al had grabbed Asher, the two of them deep in discussion fighting over some line they thought the censors would ping, and Teddy was surrounded by the Collins girls as he entertained her cousins with stories about some of his funniest/worst dates.

Owen and the other cast members were doing some last-minute rehearsing, in between calls from the crew asking them to stand in various places so the lighting and camera angles could be checked.

"This is very exciting."

Fiona glanced at her mother and rolled her eyes. "You do stuff like this nearly every night, setting up the stage for your concerts."

Teagan grinned sheepishly. "Maybe, but for some reason this feels different. Probably because I'm on the sidelines and able to enjoy the frenetic energy without having any responsibilities."

"That makes sense."

"Your dad and I are so proud of you, Fee. Proud of the woman you've become. I used to worry all the time about you and your sister, about your unconventional childhood and whether or not it was right to keep you gallivanting all over the country on that bus with tutors instead of giving you a real home."

"I had the best life ever, Mom." Fiona knew Ailis hadn't always felt the same, but considering her willingness to hop back on a bus with Hunter, she suspected she was singing a different tune now.

"You've always been so confident and strong. Always known where you wanted to go. You know, you told Pop that you were going to be a storyteller when you were just five years old."

"I did?" Fiona didn't remember that.

"Yep. He reminded me of it this afternoon."

"I always thought my future plans were to be a princess."

Teagan laughed. "That's what you told us. But when you were with Pop, it was a storyteller."

It made a weird sort of sense to Fiona that she'd only tell Pop Pop the most secret desire of her heart. She looked across the pub and found him at his usual spot at the bar. One of the makeup artists was laughing loudly and powdering his face as he regaled her with a story of his own. She may not have been in Baltimore often, but that didn't mean Pop Pop hadn't made a lasting impression on her.

"I better go check on him," Fiona said, suddenly wanting the comfort only her granddaddy could provide. "Make sure he's ready for his sitcom debut."

Fiona walked across the room to him, knowing there was another secret desire in her heart, and right now, Pop Pop was the only one she could tell.

The makeup artist had just walked away when she reached him.

"You look very handsome."

"Never thought I'd be wearing makeup at my age." He didn't appear to mind though. That was the best thing about Pop Pop. He viewed every day as a blessing and every new experience as an adventure.

"Or starring in a sitcom?"

He chuckled. "Not sure one line makes me the star."

She climbed onto the stool next to him. "You'll steal the show. Even Owen says so."

"Well, we'll see. I suspect if nothing else, everyone around here will be glad my time in the spotlight is over. I think I might be annoying them a wee bit, practicing that line."

Fiona laughed as he gave her a wink that proved he knew he'd gone overboard on the rehearsing.

"Now, why don't you tell me what's going on in here?" Pop Pop asked, tapping the side of her head lightly. "Or better yet, in here," he continued, as he pointed to her heart.

"I think I made a mistake."

Pop Pop waited for her to elucidate.

"I agreed to something I'm not comfortable with, and I don't know how to change my mind."

"That's easy. You say 'I changed my mind.'"

"Even if it hurts someone or disappoints them?"

"Even then. Because lying doesn't fix things. It's the coward's way out. And you, my fair Fiona, are not a coward."

"Again with the fair." Pop Pop had called her his fair Fiona for as long as she could remember. And while she knew he meant it in the "pretty" sense, she always joked that she lacked the fairness gene.

"You're still no better at sharing, I see."

She laughed until she realized her grandfather knew exactly what they were talking about. "I'm not," she whispered. "I'm terrible at it."

He laughed. "Which young man—"

"Places on the set!" the director yelled.

Fiona looked around and sighed.

Pop Pop patted her cheek affectionately. "We'll finish this talk afterward."

She grinned. "Break a leg."

Fiona was halfway back to Sunday's Side, where she, her parents, Asher, Teddy and a handful of other people planned to watch as much of the action as they could. Before she made it, Owen caught her around the waist. He tugged her toward him for a hug and a quick kiss that was more friendly than romantic, but a shock either way, considering he hadn't touched her since returning from Hollywood.

"What was that for?" she asked.

"For luck." His smile covered his face, and it was infectious.

"You've lost your mind since that audition."

He laughed loudly. "I'm just happy." He raised his arms in the air like he'd just gone twenty rounds with Ali. "I am the king of the world."

Fiona was starting to worry about what would happen if Owen didn't get the part. He was downright giddy.

She rolled her eyes as she walked away, then took her place next to Asher and her parents. Asher was frowning. It was clear he'd just watched her exchange with Owen, but she wasn't sure why that would make him mad.

She was surprised again when Asher placed a hand on her waist, tugging her closer to him. Then he left his hand there, even when it was obvious her dad was watching them.

"What?" he asked when she gave him a narrow-eyed glance.

"Thought you forgot about me."

He winced, flashing her a guilty smile. "Can we talk tonight after the show? You, me and Owen?"

For the first time, she noticed that Asher didn't appear to have been sleeping either. The dark circles had been hidden by his glasses, as had the stress lines in the corners of his eyes. Even so, how had she missed that?

Too preoccupied by her own anxiety.

She nodded. "Yeah. We need to talk."

His frown returned. Wow. He wasn't looking forward to this conversation either. She tried not to read too much into it, tried to ignore the piecing pain in her chest that warned she was about to get her heart broken.

"Fiona—" Asher started.

But the director yelled out again, "Quiet on thc set!"

For the next two hours, she and Asher stood together, watching the finale unfold and, despite the apprehension of what was going to come after the show, they laughed with everyone else, delighted to see their words translated so beautifully when spoken by talented actors.

Before they reached the last scene—with Pop Pop's big line—her parents leaned toward them, declaring it the best *Wild Winters* show yet.

All of them tried to press closer as the director yelled "action!" to start rolling on the last scene. The bedraggled cast was sitting exhaustedly around a table in the center of the pub—Owen with one shoe on, per the storyline—when a man dressed in a bear costume walked in.

Pop Pop stood up and delivered his line perfectly.

"Hey, did anybody call for a singing bear?"

"Cut," the director said, "and that's a wrap!"

Everyone in the room erupted in joyous laughter.

Tris and Padraig came out from behind the bar, slapping Pop Pop on the back. Her cousins rose from their various places around the bar, chattering nonstop about how amazing the experience had been.

The noise level in the bar was insane, but that wasn't obvious until it died suddenly as music unexpectedly started playing, and all the TV screens in the bar—which had been showing prerecorded sporting events—flashed to white.

Fiona recognized the song instantly, and her first thought was "ugh" as Justin Timberlake's "That Girl" started playing. For one thing, the song was too slow for the current celebratory atmosphere, and for another, Brock—the biggest JT fan in the world—had declared this was "their song" one night at a charity function as they danced together. Personally, she would have picked something—anything—else, and she'd decided then and there his JT devotion was unnatural and annoying.

Then she realized there was something showing on all the televisions. Pictures of her and…

"Oh fuck," she muttered.

Asher was still standing next to her, but Fiona couldn't find the courage to look in his direction.

She didn't have to. She knew from his softly murmured, "shit," he was watching the show as well.

Photo after photo of her and Brock flashed before her as "their song" played.

Owen walked over, frowning as he looked around the room. "Where is he?"

Fiona glanced from Owen to Asher. "He's supposed to be in Dubai until May."

Teddy stepped next to Owen, shaking his head in disgust. "Fucking Mr. Big Gesture."

None of them noticed the bear had moved closer to them until a furry paw reached out, touching Owen on the shoulder to move him aside.

Fiona watched in fascinated horror as the bear dropped to one knee in front of her, a ring box in his other furry hand.

"No," she whispered as he pushed off the large, ridiculous-looking bear head and popped open the box. "Brock."

He was wearing the same cocky smile he pulled out every time he went for the big gesture. She took note of the confidence in his expression, his assuredness that this time he'd topped them all. There was no doubt in his eyes that this gesture, like all the others, would win her back.

As the last strains of the song faded, Fiona looked up at the TV to see a live feed. Clearly Brock was in cahoots with one of the cameramen, because her face at that moment was being projected for the entire pub to see.

She looked back down at Brock, shaking her head slowly. The idiot was too proud of himself to recognize the horror on her face.

"I called Al right after Valentine's Day," Brock started. This was always his favorite part. Explaining how he'd managed to pull off the big surprise. "He and I cooked up this scheme with a lot of the crew members." He looked around, giving a couple of the cameramen the thumbs-up.

Fiona's hands clenched into fists as she felt the unnerving desire to punch her ex-boyfriend's lights out. Had he always been this obnoxious with his gestures, or was he just getting too accustomed to her falling for them?

"Brock," she said louder, hoping to halt the rest.

It was pointless. He was on a roll.

"Fiona Adams. I'm hoping that here, in the presence of your family and our friends, you'll make me the happiest man alive by agreeing to marry me."

Fiona didn't reply. She was too busy dissecting the proposal, trying to figure out who here was his friend, and sarcastically acknowledging that a marriage to her wasn't going to impact his happiness in any way. Then she focused on what he didn't say.

He didn't say "I love you."

Chapter Thirteen

Asher stood next to Fiona, fighting every impulse that told him to pick Brock up off the floor by the scruff of his outrageous costume and lay him out with a hard right to the jaw.

The only reason he didn't was because this was Fiona's battle, and she wouldn't thank him for interfering.

But why hadn't she said "no" immediately?

Owen, obviously, had the same thought, and he wasn't as good at reining in his knee-jerk reaction to surprises. "You've gotta be fucking kidding me. Fee, you can't seriously be considering this proposal?"

Brock shot Owen a dirty look, offended by his interruption to what was obviously a well-rehearsed line. "You need to take a couple of steps back, orphan boy."

Brock's angry retort was the equivalent of ringing a bell to start the round.

Teddy started toward Brock, his fists clenched. "Don't you dare talk to him like that! Who the fuck do you think—"

Owen turned and held back Teddy, who was coming in hot, before he started swinging. "Forget it, Ted."

"Forget it?" This time it was Fiona's enraged question filling the silence of the pub. Asher hadn't noticed the pin-drop quietness until that moment. "*What* did you call him?" she asked Brock, who'd pushed himself up off the floor, smartly seeking higher ground, considering the number of pissed-off people currently circling him.

"You're going to defend *him*?" Brock asked, gesturing to Owen. "After he just ruined my marriage proposal? Fiona, this was going to be one of the most special days of our lives and that idiot just destroyed it."

"Special day? Are you *insane*? I broke up with you, Brock!"

The man's utter confusion probably wasn't completely his fault. After all, Fiona had sort of mastered the art of breaking up with Brock, then backsliding. "I thought…"

"You thought you'd sweep in here as Mr. Big Gesture, throw a ring on my finger and all would be well again. And the fact you genuinely believed that would work is my fault. I'm going to own up to that, because in the past, I've let the trips and the serenade and the roses and wine work. But those things don't make a relationship, Brock. Love doesn't work like this. Five minutes of wow accompanied by five years of nothing."

"Fiona—" Brock started as her words appeared to have hit their mark.

"Do you love me?"

It was the same question Fiona said she'd asked him on Valentine's Day. And his tired tone had told her the truth.

Brock's three-second hesitance appeared to answer her question more truthfully than his "yes, of course."

"I can't marry you, Brock. I've fallen in love with—"

"Wait," Owen interjected loudly. "Wait a second, Fee. I need to say something."

"No. I do." Asher had held his tongue, giving Fiona the space she needed, but he couldn't let them fall any deeper down the rabbit's hole.

"What's going on?" Brock asked, looking from Owen to Asher. "You mean…you're in love with…"

Brock's gaze landed on Teddy, probably looking for an answer to which one, but as always, Teddy managed to take the heaviest of moment and turn it into pure humor. "Don't look at me. I think Fee is great, but my compass points in a different direction."

If Asher had played the next five minutes out in his head a thousand different ways, he never, not once, would have landed on what actually happened.

Teddy jerked his head toward Owen. "It points in *his* direction."

Owen rolled his eyes, laughing. "Jesus, Ted. This is how we're going to tell them? Your timing sucks, babe."

Brock was forgotten as Asher looked at Owen and Teddy, his best friends, his college roommates, his colleagues, the men he thought he knew as well as he knew himself—and felt his jaw drop.

"*What?*" At least Fiona was capable of speech.

Asher wasn't sure he'd find his voice again in a century.

"I'm really sorry, Fee. I know you and Asher had your hearts set on the three of us being together. I never should have… I feel terrible for letting you both think…"

Teddy shook his head. "You suck at talking about emotions, Owen."

"Shut up, Teddy," Owen replied, his tone pure affection despite the words.

"What's going on here?" Brock asked. "Fiona? Have you been cheating on me all this time?"

That was it. Asher threw the punch before he had two seconds to think about his actions.

One second Brock, Mr. Big Gesture, was accusing Fiona of cheating, the next, he was laid out on the floor.

"Fiona is the most honest woman you'll ever meet, and the fact that you just questioned her proves you don't know her at all."

"That's it!" Brock crab-crawled away from him. "The four of you are fucking crazy. You deserve each other."

Al walked over to help Brock up. Asher didn't fail to notice none of the Collins men did. They were all scowling at Brock, who ripped off the bear costume and stormed out without another word.

Fiona bent over and picked up the jeweler's box. "He forgot his ring."

Asher took it out of her hand and passed it over to Al. "You mind giving that to your buddy?"

Al paled, and Asher instantly regretted flashing the latent anger in the other man's direction. "I thought they were still…I never would have…"

Asher calmed instantly. "I'm sorry, Al," he said.

At the same time, Fiona assured, "It's not your fault. It's mine. Past history and all that."

It was time for the four of them to get out of there. They'd gone from comedy to melodrama in the blink of an eye, and there were at least fifty witnesses in the pub. Mercifully, more than half were part of the Collins clan, so perhaps they could minimize the gossip.

Al turned around and gestured for the crew to stop gaping and start breaking down the set.

Half of Fiona's family gave them all encouraging smiles as they headed out, either to the apartment upstairs or their own homes in the neighborhood; the other half kept milling around just in case anything else exciting happened.

Fiona drifted over to speak to her mother, which left him, Teddy and Owen with her grandfather.

"You boys sure do know how to put on a show. That was a fine time."

Asher tilted his head, feeling fairly confident he knew what *show* the old guy was talking about. "You're not talking about *Wild Winters*, are you?"

Patrick chuckled. "No, son. I'm not. You three okay with the way this shook out?"

Asher saw Owen's gaze drift over to Fiona, and he realized there was still a lot to say.

"We will be, Mr. Collins," Teddy said.

"Now, now. What did I say about that? It's Pat, my boy. Why don't you and I have a drink at the bar and get to know each other? Leave these two to sort out the particulars."

Teddy smiled, clearly pleased by the invite. "Finally. A hot Collins man offering to buy me a drink and show me a good time. You two clowns take your time. I'm in good hands."

Patrick laughed loudly. "There he is. Everyone kept swearing you were a hoot, but…" The rest of Patrick's words were lost to Asher as the two men walked away.

He and Owen stared at each other a full minute before Asher broke the standoff.

"What the hell, man?"

Owen ran his hand through his hair, a sure sign he was nervous. "I haven't been honest with you. Or Fee. Or Teddy. Hell…I haven't been honest with myself."

"So, this thing between you and Teddy…I'm not losing my mind, right? It wasn't always there?"

Owen shook his head. "My feelings were. But no, I didn't come clean to him until after the audition on Tuesday."

"What did he say?"

Owen grinned. "You know Teddy. He made some joke about preferring you, but being okay with settling for me. Then he kissed me, and I knew that joke didn't hold a bit of truth."

"He was always in love with you too." Asher started thinking back over the last year or two, remembering the signs. So many times, Asher had thought Owen was jealous of Teddy's active love life, when in reality, he was jealous of Teddy's lovers.

"So, all the Ashleys and Brittanys and…"

"Just dates. No sex. They liked being seen with a TV star. I was all talk."

"What about our senior year? You got drunk and said Fiona was the only woman you'd ever love."

"I meant that. It's true. I do love her. But I'm not *in* love with her. I wanted to tell you, man, but…"

"Why now, Owen?"

Owen paused, and Asher could tell it was a question he'd expected, anticipated. "I'm trying to make it in Hollywood, Ash, trying to make my mark as a leading man, the heartthrob."

Asher understood that. Knew how much Owen loved acting, loved his life as a TV star and how he longed to go further, to make an even bigger mark. "So what changed that? Because Teddy just outted you to the whole cast and crew."

"We'd already talked about it. We were going to tell you and Fiona first and then…just let it filter out the rest of the way. I'm not hiding anymore. I can't."

"Doesn't really answer my question. Why did you agree to be part of a threesome with me and Fee if—"

"I'm so sorry about that, Ash. I really am. I wouldn't have done that if you hadn't…"

Asher recalled that night after karaoke. "I forced your hand."

"It's going to sound so fucked up, but I kept thinking…if I can't have the best friend I really want, what would be so wrong about being with the other two? I never lied. The three of you are my family. You're all I have. I'd do anything to keep us together, to make sure…"

Owen's words kept fading. Teddy was right. Owen struggled to express his feelings, but tonight, right now, he was saying more than Asher had ever heard, ever realized. He didn't have to finish the sentences.

"We're solid, Owen. Always have been. Always will be."

"You and Fiona are perfect together."

Asher nodded, praying Fiona felt the same way, that she would be okay without the package deal.

Then Owen rubbed his chin, lifting his shoulder in a way that screamed guilt. "Hope you don't mind, but I was telling Teddy about last weekend. He was hoping you could teach me some of that alpha-male stuff."

Asher rolled his eyes even as he laughed. "Don't take this the wrong way, Owen, but those lessons would probably be more successful if I gave them to Teddy."

Owen's eyes widened. "Oh! Yeah. I could get on board with that."

Owen glanced toward Fiona, and Asher followed his gaze. She was still talking to her parents, probably trying to explain… Jesus. Asher didn't have a clue what she was telling them.

"You mind if I talk to Fee alone for a couple of minutes?" Owen asked. "I'd like a chance to apologize."

Asher put his hand on Owen's shoulder. "Sure thing. I'll go hold up the bar with Teddy and Pat."

***

Fiona looked over as Asher went to join Pop Pop and Teddy at the bar. Owen gave her a sheepish grin and she closed her eyes, unable to hide her own smile. She excused herself. "I need to go talk to the guys, Mom."

Mom hugged her. "That really was quite a show."

She laughed at her mom's joke, hugged her dad and said good night, watching as they left the pub to head back for the bus, hand in hand.

"Can we find somewhere quiet to talk for a few minutes?" Owen asked, walking over to her.

She nodded and pointed to a booth on Sunday's Side. While there were quite a few people still breaking down the makeshift set on the pub side, the restaurant was relatively quiet.

The past few days she'd suffered a never-ending mix of exhaustion and anxiety culminating into…Jesus…whatever tonight was. She still hadn't quite wrapped her head around Owen and Teddy as a couple. That was going to take some time.

Owen followed her into the booth, sharing the same seat.

She opened her mouth to speak, to ask him what the hell was going on, but he beat her to the punch.

"I think we were right to break it off the first time."

"I know."

Owen didn't seem surprised by her admission, which made her wonder if Asher would be. She'd been running on fumes for days, and the things that had been bothering her seemed less likely now than they had a few hours ago. Hell, the last year or so suddenly seemed clearer.

Owen picked up a napkin from the table, fiddling with it nervously. "I should never have agreed to go to your bedroom the night of that party. Time has a way of making you forget things. I don't think either of us intended to break things off that night at school. The whole thing just fell apart in a flash of red-hot anger. It was a big fight, followed by a couple quiet weeks and then, boom, we were friends again. And our friendship was better after the breakup because the couple stuff didn't work for us. The friendship was stronger than the relationship."

"It was," she whispered.

"So, we let the love we feel for each other as friends overshadow the truth—that we just didn't work together as a couple."

She nodded, closing her eyes against the tears forming. While his words matched everything she felt, that didn't mean she didn't feel sad hearing them.

"If you knew that, why did you agree to the threesome?"

Owen ran his hand through his hair. "Asher sort of backed me into a corner after karaoke, telling you that he wanted you, and that I did too. It's not that I don't love you, Fee. God. You're the only girl I've ever loved. I mean that. With all my heart. And, well, if I was ever going to go for a ménage, there's no question I'd want it to be with Asher and—"

"Teddy." She giggled. All this time, she'd been worried about hurting his feelings, while he'd been trying to spare hers.

Owen laughed, then nodded. "Sorry."

"So much for being the center of your universe."

He gave her a serious look. "Do you want to be?"

She shook her head. "No."

"Because you know you're the center of Asher's. And he's the center of yours."

Owen wrapped his arm around her shoulders, and she curled into him, sighing.

She closed her eyes, enjoying the closeness they still shared after fearing it would be lost.

"You and Asher are good together. I never really wondered about it because Brock was always there, but these past few days…I started thinking about things."

"What do you mean?"

"You always stuck with Brock because of the big gestures, right? And it never worked out."

She nodded. "Right."

"Because Brock couldn't do the little things, the things that actually add up to big. Asher does those for you. All the time. He stops at Starbucks every damn morning to get your favorite coffee, even though he doesn't drink the pricy stuff. Idiot is happy with the cheap shit in Al's coffeepot that's strong enough to walk out of the studio itself."

She crinkled her nose and nodded in agreement.

Owen continued, "We had to stop by your apartment on the way to the airport for your sweater, because you mentioned Baltimore was chilly and warned us to pack better than you had. Hell, Asher even knew which one was your favorite sweater. I swear to God, I've never seen that thing he brought you."

Fiona rolled her eyes. "I wear it every damn day."

"See?" he said, as if she'd merely proven his point. "Plus, he always fixed all the shit in your apartment when Brock was out of town."

Fiona considered that, then added, "When Brock was in town too."

Owen shook his head, looking at her like she was a fool. And he was right. The answer was obvious, and it had been in front of her eyes all this time.

But she'd never admitted she was wrong easily. "In my defense, he was in a relationship until New Year's."

Owen snorted. "That thing between him and Christina was never a relationship. It was sex, pure and simple. Really kinky, hot sex, but sex just the same."

"Remind me to call her when we get back to Cali and thank her. She's one hell of a teacher."

"You're not kidding. Damn. I might call her too." Owen pulled his arm away, and then apparently missed touching her, because he reached for her hand as he propped his feet on the bench seat on the other side.

"So…you and Teddy?" she asked.

Owen's smile lit up his whole face the second she said Teddy's name. "Watching you and Asher together sort of…"

"What?" she prompted.

"Shook something loose in me. Not sure I know how to explain it."

When several minutes passed, she understood he really couldn't find the words to describe his feelings.

Finally, he said, "There's something to be said for falling in love with your best friend. You and Asher did that."

"And you wanted the same?"

"I was already there. I've been in love with Teddy for a while now. I just…didn't know how to admit it. To him. To myself."

"The other night, when we were dancing…you had a…" She looked down, gesturing without words at his cock.

Owen actually flushed. "I got a little hot and bothered watching Teddy doing that bump and grind with the bonbon. Had to use you as a shield. Sorry about that."

"And that kiss under the mistletoe at Christmas?"

"Well," Owen rubbed his jaw guiltily. "I owe you an apology for that too. Teddy had spent the whole morning talking about his hookup the night before, and it got under my skin. I was trying to make him jealous."

Fiona was always amazed how two people could view the exact same moment in completely opposite ways. Perspective was a playful bitch who always got the last laugh.

"These past few days, I thought you were happy because of the audition. It had nothing to do with that, did it?"

Owen shook his head. "Don't get me wrong. It went well, and I think I have a really good shot at the role, but no…I was happy because I came out to Teddy. Told him I loved him, and he said it back."

Fiona gave in to her exhaustion and the emotions and let the tears fall. "I'm so happy for you. For both of you." She swiped at her eyes.

Owen seemed to need more convincing. "So those are good tears?"

She nodded. "The best."

"Did I mess things up for you and Ash?"

"No," Fiona rushed to reassure him, hoping she was telling him the truth. Even if it may be a lie, she wasn't going to let Owen spend one second worrying about it. What happened next was up to her and Asher.

Colm walked over to their booth. "Hey, have either of you seen Sunnie?"

Fiona shook her head. "No. Not since the taping. Why?"

Colm gave her a shit-eating grin as he glanced at Owen. "She owes me twenty bucks. I won that bet. My money was on Asher." He walked toward the kitchen, still on the hunt.

Fiona laughed, but didn't have time to explain to a confused Owen before Asher peeked around the doorway and spotted them in the booth. "Everything good?"

They nodded and Owen stood, helping her out. He held out his arms and she stepped into his embrace.

"I love you, Fee."

"I love you too, Owen."

He gave her one of his sweet, gentle, friendly kisses, and then he walked back to the pub in search of Teddy, slapping Asher on the back as he went by.

"I think you and I should have a talk," Asher said.

Fiona nodded. This talk was four days overdue.

"Okay, but before we head out…Happy Clam wants to know if she's going to be a part of this discussion."

Asher laughed. "I can talk to her first if you think it would help."

Fiona blew out a relieved breath. As far as she was concerned, they'd just had their talk. "She's kind of a needy bitch that way."

He shook his head. "How long are you going to make me talk about your vagina in third person?"

"You two heading out?"

Fiona looked over her shoulder, delighted when Pop Pop joined them. She gave him a hug. "Told you you'd steal the show."

"Ah, lass," Pop Pop said, still beaming, "I have to thank the two of you for that. Never in all my life thought I'd have an opportunity to be on a TV show. Sunday would have loved it. Twenty dollars says she would have wanted to be one of those extras up there singing karaoke in the background, and *then* you would have seen someone steal the show. Your mother got her beautiful voice from Sunday."

Fiona smiled when Pop Pop mentioned the grandmother she'd never met. It occurred to her that while Grandma Sunday died before she was born, she'd always felt like a real person, like someone Fiona knew, simply because Pop Pop kept her alive with his memories. "I would have loved to hear that."

Pop Pop smiled wistfully, then realized they'd been on their way out. "Oh dear. I'm keeping you two, aren't I? Going back to the hotel tonight, my fair Fiona?"

She nodded.

"It looks like you both got what you wanted in the end. I had a feeling things might turn out okay. I'll leave you to the fun stuff then." With that, he turned to join Riley, who was waiting to drive him home. Like Pop Pop, Aunt Riley was still grinning from ear to ear, exhilarated by the crazy night.

Fiona gave Asher a curious look. "Both of us?"

"Come on. Maybe I *should* talk to you before Happy Clam."

Chapter Fourteen

Asher grasped Fiona's hand and led her out of Pat's Pub. For a split second, he considered guiding her toward the waterfront, thinking they'd stand a better chance of talking if they weren't within five feet of a bed. Then he changed his mind. He knew what he wanted to say, and he knew where he wanted to be when he said it. And it was in the damn bed.

"That was quite a night," he started. "Sort of feels like life imitated art there. The Anything Goes theme slipping off the page and the stage and into reality."

"You can say that again. I can't believe Brock showed up. Or that he wore that stupid bear costume. I had to beg to get him to be Danny Zuko to my Sandy one year for Halloween. All he had to do was cuff his damn jeans and wear a leather coat. You would have thought I'd asked him to shave his head and walk around naked."

Asher wished he was at a place where he could laugh about Brock's big gesture, but he wasn't there yet. "When I saw those pictures of the two of you flashing on every TV in the place..."

Fiona tugged his hand to stop him in place. He turned to face her, taking her other hand in his as she said, "Ancient history."

"Two months ago isn't that ancient."

"It feels like a million years ago to me. Brock doesn't exist in my world anymore. I swear."

"He proposed, Fee. You said you wanted to get married just a week ago."

She huffed out an exasperated breath that told him she found his comment completely ridiculous. It was a very comforting sound. "Not to *him*! I think you're missing the most important part of the whole night. The last big gesture came…"

"And you resisted."

She smiled. "Big gestures aren't where it's at."

Asher wrapped his arm around her shoulders and they started walking toward the hotel again. "Out of vogue, huh?"

"Totally."

"What's in then?" he said, enjoying their easy banter.

"Hopefully Biggus Dickus in about," she reached for her phone to check the time, "five minutes?"

He picked up the pace, the two of them laughing as they ran the last fifty feet to the hotel. Walking through the automatic doors, they fell into each other the second the elevator doors closed. Asher kissed her hard and hungrily, unwilling to give up the close proximity, her warmth or the sweet, clean scent of her hair even when the doors parted on their floor.

They walked, awkwardly, still kissing as he pushed her backwards down the hallway. Thank God it was the middle of the night and no one was around.

If felt amazing to have her lips on his again. He'd felt okay about where they stood on Thursday morning…the two of them still wandering around in a sexual haze, riding the last waves of complete satiation.

Then Owen came back, and too many days passed without touching or kissing or talking, and the doubts started to creep in. He wasn't sure why. He'd kept his distance initially because he was hoping to grab some time alone with Owen to talk about their failed attempt at a ménage, but the right time never came. One day became two, and then three, and by then, he'd lost too much sleep to think clearly about anything, convinced he'd fucked up everything with Fiona irrevocably.

Asher shook the last of those insecurities away when Fiona surreptitiously reached down and pinched his ass as they finally reached the door to their suite.

"Bad girl," he said, deepening his voice in the way he knew was certain to get her juices flowing.

They walked into the hotel suite together, grinning when they noticed the door to the room Teddy and Owen had been sharing since their return to Baltimore was closed.

"Someone's getting busy over there," Fiona whispered in a singsong voice.

Asher gestured toward the other bedroom, thrilled when she walked in that direction with a saucy grin.

When he followed her in, shutting and locking the door, she giggled and said, "Someone's getting busy in here too."

"Oh yeah? No conversation?"

"Can we save it until after?"

He nodded. "I think if you want me to say anything intelligent, it will have to be after."

He put his glasses on the nightstand. Fiona perched on the edge of the mattress, but he shook his head, reaching for her arm. Asher pulled her up again, tugging her T-shirt over her head in one quick swish. The bra followed.

Fiona started unfastening her jeans, ready to steamroll through at full speed ahead. As always.

Asher swatted her hands away from her jeans. “Not so fast.”

She growled, an honest-to-God, narrow-eyed grumble that didn’t scare him a bit.

“Dirty looks aren’t going to get you what you want,” he said, his own voice suddenly deep and husky. His dick was rock-hard and currently in agreement with Fiona. For the first time, Asher had her all to himself without Owen, or the idea of him, looming in the back of Asher’s mind.

Fiona was his.

And he planned to make sure that she knew it beyond all reasonable doubt before she left this room.

He reached out to grasp her breasts, loving the way they filled his hands, her nipples budded, tight, perfect for sucking on.

The thought stimulated motion as he bent forward to take one into his mouth. Fiona gasped, then gripped his head, holding him to her.

She ran her fingers through his hair, fisting large sections and tugging. He grunted his approval even as he kept sucking.

“Doesn’t that hurt?” she whispered.

He lifted his head. “I’m like you, Fee. I don’t mind an edge of pain with the pleasure.” To prove his point, he took her other nipple in his mouth, increasing the suction until she moaned.

“God, Ash,” she whispered.

He played with her for several minutes until her panting turned to cries, and then, as always, curses and demands. He didn’t tell her that it wasn’t only *her* arousal that was reaching fever pitch. Every little mew or squeak she made had him fighting not to rip off his pants, toss her on the bed and fuck her until neither one of them could walk.

"Take off your shirt," she said, her hands moving on him, intent on following her own command. He shrugged it off, laughing when her hands returned to her jeans with haste.

Once again, he pushed them away.

"Asher—" she started.

"Fiona," he mimicked. She didn't continue to chastise him when he took over, unzipping her pants, then pushing his hands inside the denim to work them off. There was no denying her ass looked hot in tight jeans, but he wondered sometimes how she could breathe in them.

Fiona kicked off her shoes, then the pants and panties.

He could never resist the temptation to take a step back to admire. "Jesus. Beautiful." Then he added, "Mine."

The last word seemed to have a more powerful effect. She reached out to run her hand along his chest, taking her own mini-tour before lifting her eyes to his and retorting with a "mine" in a tone that dared him to contradict her.

"Prove it," he taunted.

Her eyes flashed with delight in the face of his dare. She loved a challenge.

Leaning forward, she sank her teeth into his pec, causing him to jerk back in surprise and, well…because it hurt.

He narrowed his eyes.

"Marking my territory."

"Is that how this is going to go? Fine. I wouldn't mind leaving a few marks myself."

Before she could respond to that, he sat down on the side of the mattress and flipped her over his lap.

Fiona didn't even try to push herself up. They'd toyed with spanking a few nights earlier, and if her body-racking orgasm was anything to go by, he'd say she'd loved it.

She proved that point even further when she went limp and actually sighed.

"It's obvious spanking can't be used as a punishment with you," he murmured, rubbing his hands over her ass.

She looked up at him. "Punishment?"

Asher wasn't surprised by her confusion. Fiona didn't possess an ounce of submissiveness. God help him, she was probably more alpha than he was. The fact that she viewed spankings as foreplay was a testament to that. In Fiona's mind, she was getting exactly what she wanted.

He recalled sitting with several of her uncles at that picnic many moons ago, listening to her father, Sky, and Tris trading "horror stories" about the challenges of raising their headstrong, independent children, namely Fiona and Colm. Asher had gotten a kick out of hearing some of the crazy things she had done when she was young, and the exasperation had still been evident in Sky's voice as he'd talked about her willfulness and inability to admit defeat.

Funny enough, the men had all agreed in the end that those were probably all the traits that had led to her success as an adult. And the reason why the man who fell for her would always have to be on his toes.

Asher, too much like Fiona, hadn't taken their comments as a warning. Instead, even then he'd felt the challenge behind them. Because he'd known the two of them were well suited.

"Yes," he said at last. "Punishment. For when you're naughty."

She snorted and turned her face back to the floor as if he were joking. "Yeah, right. I'd love to see you try that."

It was the worst thing she could have ever said.

Fiona was anticipating, looking forward to his sexual spanking. So he didn't give it to her. He held her in the facedown position, lightly caressing her back and her ass.

She sighed contentedly for a full sixty seconds at his soft touch.

Then she grew impatient.

"Asher," she said, thinking his name and her tone would be enough to stimulate a response.

He simply continued stroking her skin gently. In fact, he lightened the touch, barely moving his fingers and keeping them well away from the hot zone.

Fiona, queen of impatience, didn't let another thirty seconds elapse before she looked up at him again. "What the hell are you doing?"

"Touching you."

"Stop fucking around and get to the good stuff."

Asher shook his head. "No. I'm testing out a theory."

"What theory?"

"I've found your punishment. Withholding pleasure."

She pushed up and he let her, but when she started to stand, he gripped her waist and tugged her until she was sitting on his lap.

"You're pissing me off."

He chuckled and kissed away the scowl. "I know, but I can't resist. You're very used to getting your way, Fee. In pretty much everything. Sex isn't going to work that way."

"Of course it is."

Asher couldn't help it. He laughed. Her answer was pure Fiona—and he realized this wasn't a battle he wanted to wage tonight.

He wanted her.

More than that, he loved her. Completely. Which meant she was right. She was going to gct everything she desired…and if he could find a way to make it possible, even more.

He flipped her over, teasing as he called her a hopeless case and planted several slaps on her ass.

Fiona gripped his calf muscle in order to gain leverage that would allow her to lift her ass toward his down strokes. She urged him to keep going, to spank her harder. Asher did both.

Maybe it was Fiona who'd schooled him on how things would go.

She glanced up at him when a chuckle escaped.

"Funny?" she asked.

Asher shook his head, not bothering to explain. He'd tell her later. Or actually, he wouldn't. She was demanding enough already. It wouldn't work in his favor if she knew the power was in her hands, that there was nothing he wouldn't give her.

To distract her from her question, he slid his fingers between her legs, pressing two inside without preamble. She was soaking wet, her pussy on fire.

She gasped, her hips jerking toward him, moving in tandem with his thrusts.

"God, Ash. Fuck me. So ready."

He was to, but he'd already lost too much ground with her. So instead, he continued playing, his fingers dancing from clit, to pussy, to toy with her ass. He'd made the rounds a few times, always leaving her just there, hovering on the peak, without allowing her to come.

After half a dozen near misses, she started to fight to get up.

"Can't take any more. Need—"

"I know what you need." He pressed her down, holding her face down over his lap, refusing to give way.

She struggled, until he pushed one finger all the way in her anus, straight to the hilt.

Fiona reared up.

"Oh my God," she cried out loudly.

He withdrew, then returned, his finger drenched with the juices of her arousal. It eased his motion, allowed him to slide in smoothly.

When Fiona began to match his pace, he knew he'd made her a believer in anal play. He pushed her just to the edge of her orgasm, then pulled his finger out.

She went limp, the fight driven out of her.

"Ash," she whispered, her body trembling slightly. "Please."

It was all he needed to hear. He lifted her, gently laying her on her back. Shrugging off his jeans, he crawled over her, swiftly pushing inside her clenching pussy.

One thrust. That was all it took.

Fiona arched her back, crying out as she came.

Asher fucked her throughout, never slowing his pace, never giving her a chance to land. The first orgasm waned for mere seconds before the second flashed.

He prayed he'd be able to hang in there to give her a third, but in keeping her on edge, he'd pushed himself to the limit as well.

Once the second orgasm softened, her body relaxed and her eyes drifted closed.

Asher pushed in all the way and held, buried to the hilt. Then he bent lower to kiss her. Relaxed was *not* how he wanted her at the moment.

He stroked her clit, sparking an immediate response. Her eyelids flew open and she shook her head. "I can't take another one of those," she said, the words labored as she struggled to catch her breath.

"Of course you can. You're going to. Next one is with me, okay?"

She nodded, though she looked far from convinced of her abilities.

Unable to resist, he kissed her again. Fiona's tongue touched his, and he recognized a renewed energy in her. He let the kiss linger as he played with her clit, using that sensitive spot to rouse her, to bring her back into the game.

When her hips started to rise and fall, seeking more pressure, he gave her—them—exactly what they wanted.

A hard, frenzied, amazing fuck.

Asher had never taken a woman with such reckless abandon, but Fiona made it easy.

Hell, she made it necessary. Her nails scored his shoulders as she yelled at him to "go harder" and "faster," even when neither was possible.

One hard touch to her clit sent her over a third time, and he gave in and took the leap with her.

His hips jerked as come erupted, filling her. They held there, him above her, the two of them breathing heavily, their bodies slick with sweat as they tried to recover.

He dropped next to her, aware neither of them would be able to sleep in their current states. The room felt like it was the temperature of a sauna, thanks to their exertions.

"Shower?" she asked.

"Sounds perfect. I'm a sweaty mess."

They walked naked to the bathroom, Asher wondering if he could convince her to move to a nudist colony with him. Her body was too beautiful to hide beneath clothing.

Together, they took the world's steamiest shower, something that had very little to do with the lukewarm temperature of the water and everything to do with Fiona dropping to her knees and taking his cock in her mouth. So much for cooling off.

As they took turns drying each other, Asher realized there was still one thing left to say. "You asked me the other night about the advice your Pop Pop and uncle had given me, remember?"

She nodded, wrapping the towel around herself. "I forgot about that. So much has happened since then."

"I know. I still haven't taken their advice."

"What is it?"

"To tell you this." He reached for her, pulling her into his arms and kissing her with all the love he felt in his heart. Fiona's arms were around his neck in an instant.

When they parted, he placed his hands on her cheeks and held her gaze. "I love you, Fiona Adams. So much it hurts. There's nothing I wouldn't give you, wouldn't do for you. Except—"

"Share," she whispered.

He closed his eyes and sighed. "You're mine."

"I want you. Just you. Only you."

She said it three times, three different ways, and Asher let the words soak in deep.

"It's always been you for me," she admitted. "I'm not sure why it took me so long to realize. I guess we just had to get through those Brock and Christina years, right?"

"So much wasted time," he murmured as she laughed.

"Thought we were calling it experience?"

He shook his head. "Five fucking years. Wasted."

She reached for him again the same time his arms opened for her. Fiona was the first to pull away, and it was clear there was something else on her mind. He started to point to the bedroom, issuing one of those deep-voiced commands that never seemed to fail to get her engine revving.

Asher was glad he let her speak first, because he was obviously thinking with his dick while she was thinking with her heart.

"You really love me?"

He rolled his eyes. "You're not actually questioning that, are you?"

She shook her head. "No. It's just nice to hear…without having to prompt, you know?"

He did. Brock didn't offer the words freely. He waited until she asked for them, until she said enough is enough, and then he made a big fucking show of it, something worthy of bragging about to his rich friends.

What Asher didn't tell Fiona was, he'd never said those three little words before. Not even to Christina.

Fiona said it had always been him. Well, the same was true for her. He'd fallen for her at eighteen, and he didn't doubt he'd still be this deep in love with her at eighty.

"I'm not sure love feels like a strong enough word," he whispered.

Fiona wasn't a crier. Not really. He'd seen her tears a handful of times, and most of those were prompted by equal parts sadness and anger.

These were real and genuine and beautiful.

"I didn't think this much emotion was possible." Fiona swiped at her eyes, obviously embarrassed.

He tugged her hand away, then pressed his forehead to hers. He closed his eyes a split second after her and the two of them just stood there, heads pressed together, soaking in the joy of being in love, of being together.

"Can we go to bed again?" she asked, letting her towel drop to the floor.

Asher didn't reply as he took a long, appreciative look at her. Then, he bent down and picked her up.

She squealed, then laughed as he carried her back into the bedroom. "How very Rhett Butler of you."

He ruined—or improved—the effect when he tossed her onto the bed. She'd only bounced once before he was there, climbing over her, kissing her. They were already naked, but for the first time, he noticed Fiona wasn't in a mad dash for the finish line.

They kissed for weeks.

Then they took a hundred years to touch.

And then they made love forever.

When the sun peeked through the blinds, they finally rested, both lying on their sides, facing each other, holding hands.

"It's crazy how long it took us to open our eyes and see this. I mean," she said, "we've been right in front of each other all along. And the same goes for Teddy and Owen—how could they not see they were perfect for each other too? All of us were blind fools."

"Or April fools?" he asked as he gave her a playful wink.

"Well, no more," she said, in that authoritative, nothing-can-stop-her, self-assured Fiona tone. "From now on, it's you and me, Teddy and Owen—"

"Happy Clam, a trio of lightsabers, California sunshine, *Wild Winters*."

"Tequila and cotton candy."

He rolled his eyes, even as he said, “A whole lifetime of Anything Goes.”

“Starting now,” she said with a giggle, as she pushed him to his back and climbed on top.

Epilogue

"We're leaving in a few hours, Pop Pop. I wanted to stop by to tell you goodbye."

Fiona sat with Pop Pop in his large room in Riley's house. He'd moved in with her over a decade earlier, more for the peace of mind of his children than due to the fact he couldn't take care of himself.

The room was brightly lit with a large window, and he had a comfortable sitting area with two plush chairs facing his own TV.

One wall, her favorite wall, was covered with picture frames containing photos of everyone in the Collins family. The pictures were never the same, Pop Pop updating them as they grew older and, in the case of Caitlyn, Ailis, and Padraig, changing them from single shots to those of couples.

She stood up to look at the more recent photos of Caitlyn with her boyfriend, Lucas, and Ailis and Hunter backstage at one of his concerts. Her breath caught when she spotted a lovely one of Padraig and Mia together. It made her smile even as tears gathered in her eyes.

Pop Pop stepped next to her. "Love never dies," he whispered, aware of which photo had captured her attention. "The people may go away, but as long as they're in our hearts, they live."

He placed his arm around her and she rested her head on his shoulder, taking his words to heart and trying to let them comfort her.

Try as she may, she worried every time one of her visits ended and she returned to California. While Pop Pop was generally healthy, it was easier for her to see that he was slowing down than it was for the others, simply because they saw him every day and the changes were gradual. Fiona was often away for months at a time. That made his aging more apparent to her.

Fiona couldn't—wouldn't—consider a life without her Pop Pop. But that didn't mean she wasn't careful to make sure she always saw him before she left to tell him she loved him.

They stood like that for a few minutes, then something caught her eye. She lifted her head from his shoulder. "Hey, where's my picture?"

Pop Pop chuckled. "Just noticed, did you? I was wondering when you'd spot it was missing."

He walked back to the small table Riley had set up in his room and retrieved a frame. "I just finished putting it back together when you got here. Didn't have a chance to hang it up again."

He handed it to her. "Maybe you'd like to do the honors."

She laughed when she saw the new picture. It was her, Teddy, Owen and Asher standing next to the bar the day after they'd filmed the finale. Owen and Asher were both sitting on stools. Fiona stood between Asher's outstretched legs, his arms wrapped around her waist as she leaned against him. They, and Owen, were all laughing. Teddy, meanwhile, was bent over in front of Owen, Incredible-Hulk style, flexing nonexistent muscles and wearing a look of pure powerful aggression.

"Oh my God. *This* is my new picture?"

Pop Pop nodded, then gestured toward the empty nail. "Yep. Want to look at it and know you're safe and sound on that other coast with your other family."

"I have a lot of family, don't I?"

"You are truly blessed, my dear."

She put the picture on the wall, straightening the frame, and then they both stood back to admire it.

"He'll treat you good, Fiona. He's honest, thoughtful, and he loves you. You picked a fine young man."

Fiona smiled as the two of them looked at Asher. Her grandfather's approval meant the world to her. "He reminds me of you. Funny and loving and kind."

Pop Pop turned quickly, and she thought she saw him bat a tear away. He walked over to the antique record player he'd insisted on bringing from the apartment above the pub, even as Riley insisted it was better suited for the dump.

"I can't believe that thing still works," she said, following him.

"I have another surprise for you," he said as he turned the player on, lifted the arm and placed it on the album. "Found this in my pile of old albums."

Fiona's eyes widened as strains of "Waltzing Mathilda" began to play. It had been her favorite as a child. "I haven't heard this in years."

She fought back a few of her own tears when Pop Pop turned and gave her a slight bow. "Fancy a turn on the floor with an ancient beast?"

Fiona was in his arms in a second, and the two of them laughed as he held her hand high enough that she could twist and twist. "I wish I had my Belle dress," she teased.

They danced to the song two more times before she left.

"I love you, Pop Pop. See you soon?"

"I'll be here awaiting your return, my fair Fiona."

Dear Reader,

I promised after the heartbreak of *Wild Devotion* that I would write something a little more lighthearted. I hope I delivered with *Wild at Heart*. Like you, I needed to laugh after the tears spent on Padraig and Mia.

Saying that, I suspect there were some of you who were anticipating this to be a happily ever after for three people because y'all know how I love my ménage stories. To you, I simply wanted to say…

APRIL FOOLS!

Enjoy *Wild at Heart*?

Please consider leaving a review.

Please enjoy this excerpt from Wild Temptation, Wilder Irish book five. Available now.

She's tied up at work...by her boss.

The last thing Lochlan wanted in a new assistant was some inexperienced, gorgeous, submissive blonde. However, a promise to a friend ensures that's exactly what he's stuck with.

May knows she's out of her league, not only in her new job, but with her boss. He makes her want things she's never considered—kinky, sensual, wicked things.

When trouble at home shows Lochlan more about her life than she wants him to see, there's no stopping the sexy protector suddenly determined to claim not only her body, but her heart as well.

Excerpt:

"May."

She turned in surprise. She hadn't heard Lochlan come in. "I…"

"Are you okay?"

May nodded. "I'm fine."

Her words prompted a scowl she couldn't understand.

"Dammit," he muttered, reaching out to her. "You aren't *fine*. Come here."

He drew her into his arms, wrapping her up in the warmest embrace of her life. Regardless of that, May couldn't relax. She tried to pull away, but his grip was iron-clad, solid.

"Hold still." Lochlan's voice was strong and deep, and there was something in those depths that called to her, made her want so much. Too much.

The tension in her shoulders gradually loosened, and she tentatively raised her own hands, placing them around Lochlan's middle, locking them at his back.

He started to slowly sway, the rocking motion soothing, peaceful. The panic attack began to ease. They remained that way for several minutes, May's muscles relaxing, her brain shutting down. It was bliss.

"That's better. Good girl," he murmured. "Just let it all go, May."

He had a way of driving away all the dark thoughts that she couldn't quite understand. He'd simply say her name, touch her, and everything vanished.

Eventually, they shifted apart. May pulled back to look up as Lochlan glanced down. The position put their faces close, their lips mere inches apart.

She wanted him to kiss her.

No, she needed him to kiss her. And there was something in his eyes, something wild and unstrained that told her he wanted the same…and more.

Her hands slid to his waist, and she gripped his shirt tightly as she fought an internal battle over whether to pull him closer or push him away.

Lochlan reached up, one hand cupping her cheek, his intent crystal clear.

He *was* going to kiss her.

Boss.

He's your boss.

She pushed back and turned toward the window once more, forcing herself to look down at the water, so she couldn't see his face in the reflection. Couldn't see how he reacted to her rejection.

She also couldn't lose her job. It was the only thing keeping her family afloat. Granted, they were all clinging to one crappy life preserver, but it was better than nothing.

"Tell me what you want, May."

"Want?" she asked, puzzled, refusing to turn and face him.

"Yes. What you want."

"I want my mom to be okay. I want Jenny to talk."

"I'm not talking about your family. I'm talking about you. Take them out of the equation. What do *you* want?"

She knew he meant something far more personal, private. She recalled her wicked fantasies of him over the past few months. His fingers gripping her hair as he kissed her roughly, the way he would push her onto his desk and take her. Or the way she would straddle his lap in his desk chair. She wanted him to tie her up in a real bed—not on her crummy couch—and take over. Take charge.

She'd spent every minute of every hour for the past five years making every single decision—from what to eat for dinner, to figuring out how they were going to pay the electric bill. She was exhausted, and she needed someone to hold the reins for just a little while. Someone to make her forget how scared and tired she was.

She pressed her forehead against the window and sighed. She couldn't tell him that. So she lied. "I don't want anything. I'm fine, Lochlan."

"That's it. I've had it."

May's head flew up in surprise at the outright anger in his voice, and then she was twisted around. She dragged her feet as he grasped her upper arm and pulled her down a short hallway on the opposite side of the living room from where the girls were staying. Lochlan opened a door to a lovely bedroom decorated in shades of blue, her favorite color.

He followed her in and then—God help her—he shut and locked the door.

"Is this your room?" she whispered.

"No. It's yours. Mine is across the hall. I have some things to say to you, and I don't want the girls to overhear."

"Okay." May looked around the room. There was a chair next to a small desk, but that was the only place to sit in the room with the exception of the bed. She should leave the chair for him, but that meant… Even this decision defeated her at the moment.

She was feeling light-headed and—

Lochlan placed his arm around her waist and led her to the bed. "Sit down before you fall down."

She didn't want him to think she was weak. "I'm fine," she repeated, trying to instill some semblance of strength into the words.

He snorted derisively. "Of course you are. You're always fine. Even when you aren't."

"What are you talking about?"

"We're not at work."

She raised her hands in a "no kidding" way, but Lochlan didn't crack a smile. Instead, he continued explaining. "When we're not at work, I'm not your boss."

May scowled. "Of course you are. You're my boss no matter where we are."

"No. Not here. Not away from the office."

"Why are you saying that?" she asked.

"You can't keep doing this, May." Lochlan continued to answer her questions with responses that didn't fit, that didn't make sense.

"Doing what?"

"Lying about your feelings. You aren't *fine*. You're miles away from that. Pretending otherwise doesn't change the truth."

"And falling apart every three seconds doesn't either. My family—"

"Needs you. I get that. But what about what *you* need?"

She looked at him, her mind going completely blank. In truth, she couldn't think of anything she needed other than the ability to take care of her mom, Chloe and Jenny.

What she wanted, of course, was another thing entirely, but she couldn't have that.

Lochlan shook his head. "You don't know what you need, do you?"

May sighed, her shoulders tight with anxiety, her head starting to ache. "I…" She slowly shook her head.

"You need a way to relieve the pressure, to get some of these bad thoughts out before you explode."

"I don't know how to do that." She rose from the bed. She needed to get out of here, grab the girls and go back to her smoky apartment and crappy couch. She needed to figure out where she was going to get the money for her mom's surgery and how to make Jenny talk again and—

Her lungs closed up.

No. What she *really* needed was air.

"I can't stay…we have to…" She walked toward the door. "I'm fine," she choked out.

Lochlan was next to her in an instant, his hand on her upper arm, turning her toward him as he pushed her against the door. "If you say the words *I'm fine* to me one more time, I'm going to turn you over my knee and spank you."

May was shocked into silence for a full thirty seconds before she could form a single word. "What?"

"You heard me. Tell me you're fine one more time, and you're going to find that skirt of yours wrapped around your waist and your body draped over my lap. You got it?"

"Wow," she whispered.

That was probably the hottest thing anyone had ever said to her in her life. More than that, it confirmed that she wasn't the only one suffering from a bad case of wicked fantasies. Lochlan wanted the same things.

Was that what had prompted her unexpected response to him? Was there something unspoken in the way he acted around her that made her want to check all her troubles at the door and disappear into him for a night…or twenty? Had his darker desires somehow kick-started these lustful dreams in her?

For the first time since dinner, his lips curled up into a grin. "Is that a good wow or are you contemplating calling 911?"

"Do I need to call 911?"

He shook his head. "I'd never hurt you, May. Never make you do anything you didn't want. You say no and it's no. No questions asked."

"I'm tired," she whispered.

Lochlan cupped her cheek once more. This time she turned her face toward the sweet touch, soaking it up. "I know you are, sweetheart."

One night.

She knew what she needed. Turned out it was the exact same thing she wanted.

"Lochlan?"

"Yeah?"

May took a deep breath and prayed she wasn't making the biggest mistake of her life.

"I'm fine."

Praise for Wild at Heart

"The characters are **realistic** and **relatable** which I think is one of the most important things in a book. Their chemistry is off the charts, making for some hot scenes." ★★★★★*Shade, Goodreads*

"This book kept me guessing, and on **the edge of my seat!** I couldn't stop reading for anything, because I just couldn't wait to see what was coming next." ★★★★★*Jennifer, Goodreads*

"No matter what you think is going to happen, **I guarantee you'll still be surprised**!"★★★★★*Viper, Goodreads*

"A great **light-hearted**, **hot**, **wow**, **oh-no-she-didn't**, fun addition to Wilder Irish, it hits all the right marks." ★★★★★*Renee, Goodreads*

"This was a fun and steamy story - **just a delight**!" ★★★★★*Tamara, Goodreads*

ABOUT THE AUTHOR

Writing a book was number one on Mari Carr's bucket list. Now her computer is jammed full of stories — novels, novellas, short stories and dead-ends. A *New York Times* and *USA TODAY* bestseller, Mari finds time for writing by squeezing it into the hours between 3 a.m. and daybreak when her family is asleep.

You can visit Mari's website at www.maricarr.com.
She is also on Facebook and Twitter.

Look for these titles by Mari Carr

Compass
Northern Exposure
Southern Comfort
Eastern Ambitions
Western Ties
Winter's Thaw
Hope Springs
Summer Fling
Falling Softly
Heaven on Earth
Into the Fire
Still Waters
Light as Air

Second Chances
Fix You
Dare You
Just You
Near You
Reach You
Always You

Sparks in Texas
Sparks Fly
Waiting for You
Something Sparked
Off Limits
No Other Way
Whiskey Eyes

Trinity Masters
Elemental Pleasure
Primal Passion
Scorching Desire

Forbidden Legacy
Hidden Devotion
Elegant Seduction
Secret Scandal
Delicate Ties
Beloved Sacrifice
Masterful Truth

Masters Admiralty
Treachery's Devotion
Loyalty's Betrayal
Pleasure's Fury
Honor's Revenge
Bravery's Sin

Wild Irish
Come Monday
Ruby Tuesday
Waiting for Wednesday
Sweet Thursday
Friday I'm in Love
Saturday Night Special
Any Given Sunday
Wild Irish Christmas
Wild Irish Box Set

Wilder Irish
Wild Passion
Wild Desire
Wild Devotion
Wild at Heart
Wild Temptation
Wild Kisses
Wild Fire
Wild Spirit

Cowboys!
Spitfire
Rekindled
Inflamed

Big Easy
Blank Canvas
Crash Point
Full Position
Rough Draft
Triple Beat
Winner Takes All
Going Too Fast

Boys of Fall
Free Agent
Red Zone
Wild Card

Clandestine
Bound by the Past
Covert Affairs
Scoring
Mad about Meg

Cocktales
Party Naked
Screwdriver
Bachelor's Bait
Screaming O

Farpoint Creek
Outback Princess
Outback Cowboy
Outback Master
Outback Lovers

June Girls
No Recourse
No Regrets

Just Because
Because of You
Because You Love Me
Because It's True

Love Lessons
Happy Hour
Slam Dunk

Madison Girls
Kiss Me Kate
Three Reasons Why

Scoundrels
Black Jack
White Knight
Red Queen

What Women Want
Sugar and Spice
Everything Nice

Individual Titles
Seducing the Boss
Erotic Research
Tequila Truth
Power Play
Rough Cut
Assume the Position
One Daring Night
Do Over

Made in the USA
Coppell, TX
26 April 2022